Sarah's CHOICE

**Center Point
Large Print**

Also by Wanda E. Brunstetter
and available from Center Point Large Print:

Brides of Lancaster County Series
A Merry Heart
Looking for a Miracle
Plain and Fancy
The Hope Chest

Indiana Cousins Series
A Cousin's Promise
A Cousin's Prayer
A Cousin's Challenge

Brides of Lehigh Canal Series
Kelly's Chance
Betsy's Return

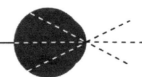

BRIDES *of* LEHIGH CANAL
BOOK THREE

Sarah's
CHOICE

WANDA E.
BRUNSTETTER

CENTER POINT PUBLISHING
THORNDIKE, MAINE

This Center Point Large Print edition
is published in the year 2010 by arrangement with
Barbour Publishing, Inc.

The text of this Large Print edition is unabridged.
In other aspects, this book may vary
from the original edition.
Printed in the United States of America
on permanent paper.
Set in 16-point Times New Roman type.

ISBN: 978-1-60285-927-2

Library of Congress Cataloging-in-Publication Data

Brunstetter, Wanda E.
Sarah's choice / Wanda E. Brunstetter. — Center Point large print ed.
p. cm.
ISBN 978-1-60285-927-2 (library binding : alk. paper)
1. Widows—Fiction. 2. Blacksmiths—Fiction. 3. Ship captains—Fiction.
  4. Lehigh Canal (Pa.)—Fiction. I. Title.
PS3602.R864S27 2011
813'.6—dc22

                                                        2010035044

Dedication/ Acknowledgments

To my husband, Richard. Thanks for all the interesting things you've shared with me about playing on the towpath and swimming in the Lehigh Canal when you were a boy.

The LORD seeth not as man seeth;
for man looketh on the outward appearance,
but the LORD looketh on the heart.

1 SAMUEL 16:7

Chapter 1

Walnutport, Pennsylvania—Summer 1898

Wo–o–o–o! Wo–o–o–o! The low moan of a conch shell drifted through the open window in Sarah Turner's kitchen.

Leaving a pan of bacon cooking on the coal-burning stove, she peered out the window. Although she saw no sign of the canal boat, the sound of its conch shell could be heard for a mile and signaled the boat would be approaching the lock soon.

"A boat's coming. Would you mind finishing the bacon while I go out to open the lockgate?" Sarah asked her mother-in-law, who stood at the counter, cracking eggs into a ceramic bowl.

"Sure, I can do that," Maria said with a weary-looking nod. A chunk of her nearly gray hair had fallen loose from the back of her bun, and her dark eyes looked dull and puffy.

Sarah's heart went out to Maria, who looked more tired than usual. Sarah feared that caring for the children was too much for her mother-in-law—especially since she'd begun having trouble with her vision.

Wo–o–o–o! Wo–o–o–o! Wo–o–o–o! The sound of the conch shell drew closer.

Sarah hurried across the room. She was almost

to the door when her eight-year-old son, Sam Jr., raced up to her, bright-eyed and smiling from ear to ear.

"Can I help raise the lock, Mama?" he asked.

Sarah shook her head. "Sorry, Sammy, but you're not strong enough for that."

"Am so strong enough! I ain't no weaklin', Mama." When the boy pulled his shoulders straight back and puffed out his chest, a lock of sandy blond hair fell across his forehead.

"Of course you're not a weakling, but raising and lowering the lock is hard work, even for me."

His blue eyes darkened as he tipped his head and looked up at her with furrowed brows. "How come ya always treat me like a baby?"

Sarah blew out an exasperated breath. "I don't treat you like a baby. I just know that you're not strong enough to raise and lower the lock. Now if you really want to help, run back to the parlor and keep an eye on your little sister and brother for me."

"Okay." Sammy thrust his hands in his pockets, turned, and shuffled out of the room.

With a shake of her head and a silent prayer for guidance, Sarah hurried outside.

As the flat-roofed wooden boat approached, she cranked open the upper wicket gates to fill the lock. Once it was filled with water, she lowered the upper head gate, and the boat was drawn into the stone walls of the lock. Then the upper head gates were raised and the upper wicket gates were closed, so that no more water could enter the lock. Next, the lower wicket gates were opened and the water rushed out of the lock. Following that, the lower gates were opened, and the boat was drawn out and into the lower level of the canal. Finally, Sarah opened the main gate to let the boat out and on its way.

As the boat moved on down the canal, Sarah headed back to the house, arms aching and forehead beaded with perspiration. This was hard work—too hard for a twenty-seven-year-old woman like her—and definitely too hard for a young boy. But she had no other choice. When her husband, Sam, died nearly a year ago, she'd taken over his job of tending the lock in order to provide for her three children.

She shuddered, thinking of the accident that had taken Sam. A boat had broken loose from where it was tied and floated to the lock, where it had jammed. Sam and several others had been trying to free the boat. While Sam was standing on top of the lock, his foot slipped, and he'd tumbled into the water. The boat shifted, and Sam's body had been crushed between the boat and the lock.

Lock tending could be dangerous work, and Sarah had to remind herself every day to be very careful in all that she did during the process of letting the boats in and out.

Sarah was grateful that Sam's mother lived with

them and had helped to care for the children ever since Sam died. But with Maria's health failing, Sarah couldn't help but worry.

She thought about her own mother, who'd died of pneumonia a few months ago. Papa had given up canaling and sold his boat soon after that. He'd moved to Easton and taken a job at one of the factories where he'd previously worked during the winter. Sarah missed seeing both of her parents, but she understood Papa's need for a change.

Sarah leaned wearily against the side of the lock tender's shed and sighed. "Oh, Sam, I miss you so much. How I wish you were still here." Tears slipped from her eyes. How many more things would change in her life? How much longer would Maria be able to help out? Could she and the children make it on their own if Maria moved back to Easton where she used to live with Sam's brother, Roger? Sarah knew that's where Maria belonged, but could she convince her of that?

"I hereby bequest to my grandson, Elias Brooks, my canal boat, with all the supplies and mules that go with it."

Twenty-eight-year-old Elias looked over at his parents to gauge their reaction to the reading of his grandfather's will. Mother, with her light brown hair pinned tightly in a bun, sat with a stoic expression on her face.

Father frowned, making his smooth, nearly bald

head stand out in contrast to the deep wrinkles in his forehead. "It won't be easy to sell that stupid boat," he said, glancing at Elias and then quickly looking away. "With the canal era winding down, I doubt the old man's boat will be worth much at all."

"How can you talk about your own father like that?" Elias's twenty-five-year-old sister, Carolyn, spoke up. "Grandpa was much more than an old man. He was your father, and a wonderful grandfather to me and Elias."

A muscle on the side of Father's neck quivered. "That man was never much of a father to me. Always thought about that ridiculous boat and how much money he could make haulin' coal up the canal from Mauch Chunk to Easton."

"It was Grandpa's money that allowed you to get the schooling you needed to run your newspaper," Elias dared to say.

Father slammed his fist on the table where they sat in Clifford Moore's law office. "How dare you speak to me like that!"

"Sorry," Elias mumbled, "but I think it's disrespectful to talk about Grandpa in such a way. He did his best by you, and—"

"His best?" Father's face flamed. "If he'd done his best, he would never have bought that boat. He'd have stayed here in Easton and helped me run the newspaper, which is where he belonged."

Mr. Moore cleared his throat a couple of times.

"Can we get back to the reading of Andrew's will?"

"You mean there's more?" The question came from Mother, who'd begun twiddling her thumbs, a gesture Elias knew indicated she was becoming quite agitated.

Mr. Moore looked at Elias. "Your grandfather also left a note saying he wanted you to have his Bible. I believe it's somewhere on the boat."

Elias nodded. He looked forward to reading Grandpa's Bible and searching for all the places he'd underlined in it. During the times Elias had spent with Grandpa when he was a boy, he'd enjoyed hearing Grandpa's deep voice as he read passages of scripture each evening before bed. It was largely due to Grandpa's godly influence that, at the age of sixteen, Elias had come to know the Lord personally. He'd been trying to live a Christian life ever since, which was why he couldn't let any of the things Father said today rile him.

Elias stared out the window as he thought about the summers during his teen years that he'd spent aboard his grandfather's boat. Father hadn't wanted Elias to go, but Mother had convinced him, saying she thought it'd be a good experience for the boy. Elias had enjoyed those days on the water, helping with various chores as Grandpa hauled load after load of coal on the Lehigh Navigation System. Grandpa hadn't expected anything from Elias except a good day's work, and he'd always offered his acceptance and praise. Not like Father, full of unreasonable demands, and critical of everything Elias said or did.

"I'll see that an ad is run in tomorrow's newspaper," Father said, bringing Elias's thoughts to a halt. "If we're lucky, someone who's still determined to haul that dirty coal up the canal might see the ad and buy the old man's boat."

Elias gripped the arm of his chair and grimaced. Grandpa deserved more respect, especially from his only son. But then, Father had never had any respect for Grandpa; at least not as far as Elias could tell.

Carolyn, her blue eyes flashing, spoke up again. "Please stop referring to Grandpa as an 'old man.'"

"I agree with Carolyn, and there's no reason for you to advertise Grandpa's boat in your newspaper either," Elias said, summoning up his courage.

Father folded his arms and glared at Elias. "Oh, and why's that?"

"Because the boat's mine, and it . . . well, it's not for sale."

Father's dark eyebrows shot up. "What?"

"Grandpa wanted me to have the boat, or he wouldn't have willed it to me." Elias loosened his collar, which suddenly felt much too tight. He wasn't used to standing up to his father like this.

"If Grandpa wanted me to have his boat, then he must have wanted me to continue hauling coal with it."

The wrinkles in Father's forehead deepened. "Wh–what are you saying?" he sputtered.

"I'm saying that I'm going to quit my job at the newspaper and captain Grandpa's boat."

Mother gasped. "Elias, you can't mean that!"

He nodded. "I certainly do."

Father's thin lips compressed so tightly that the ends of his handlebar mustache twitched up and down. "That would be a very foolish thing to do."

"I don't think it's foolish," Carolyn put in. "In fact, I think—"

Father's gaze swung to Carolyn, and he glared at her. "Nobody cares what you think, so keep your opinion to yourself!"

She blinked a couple of times, pushed a wayward strand of honey-blond hair into the tight bun she wore, and sat back in her chair with a sigh.

"Perhaps your grandfather didn't mean for you to actually captain his boat," Mother spoke up. "Maybe he left it to you so you could sell the boat and use the money for something else."

Elias's face heated, and he became keenly aware that his left cheek, partially covered by the red mark he'd been born with, felt like it was on fire. "I think Grandpa did mean for me to captain his boat. Maybe to you and Father it would be foolish for me to do so, but I feel a strong need to fulfill Grandpa's wishes."

Father's piercing blue eyes darkened like a storm cloud. "You take that boat out, and there will be no job waiting for you at my newspaper when the canal closes! Is that understood?"

Mother gasped again. "Aaron, you can't mean that!"

"Yes, Myrtle, I most certainly do." Father turned to look at Elias. "Well, what's it going to be? Are you working for me or not?"

A sense of determination welled in Elias's soul as he made his final decision. Rising from his chair, he looked his father in the eye and said, "I'm going to captain Grandpa's boat, and there's nothing you can do to stop me."

Chapter 2

"*I*'m not moving back to Easton," Maria said with a shake of her head. "You need me to care for the kids and help with things here."

Sarah dropped to a seat on the high-backed sofa beside her mother-in-law and reached for her hand. "I'm concerned because you haven't been feeling well for some time, and now that your eyesight's failing, you need to be where you can get the best medical care."

Maria's forehead puckered. "Are you sayin' that Dr. McGrath isn't giving me good care?"

"I'm not saying that at all, but there's a hospital in Easton, and doctors who specialize in—"

"I'm not leaving you to raise three kids alone, so this discussion's over." Maria rose from the sofa and shuffled across the room. When she bumped the rocking chair, she swayed unsteadily, nearly hitting her head on the fireplace mantle.

"Are you all right?" Sarah rushed to take Maria's arm.

Maria brushed Sarah's hand aside. "I'm fine. Just lost my balance for a minute, that's all." She shuffled on and disappeared into the kitchen.

Sarah groaned. "Oh, Sam, I wish you were still the lock tender and I could just be here taking care of your mother and our kids."

Elias drew in a deep breath to help settle his nerves. He and Ned Guthrie, the fifty-year-old man who'd been Grandpa's helper for the last several years, were heading up the Lehigh Navigation System in Grandpa's old boat. Ever since they'd left Easton, Elias had been a ball of nerves. He'd found a twelve-year-old boy, Bobby Harrison from Easton, to drive the mules, but Bobby didn't have a lot of experience around mules. Between that concern, and the fact that Elias hadn't ridden on Grandpa's canal boat for nearly ten years, he wondered if he'd be able to comply with Grandpa's wishes and actually run the boat himself. Well, he couldn't quit now and return to Easton, where Father would only say "I told you so."

Elias glanced at Ned, who stood at the bow of the boat, hollering at Bobby to keep the lines steady. The rusty canaler with a scruffy-looking brown beard might be a bit rough around the edges, but he'd been working the canal a good many years and had plenty of experience in all aspects of it.

It's a good thing, too, Elias thought, *because I can't remember much of what Grandpa taught me.*

As Elias's boat drew closer to the lock at Walnutport, Ned lifted the conch shell to his lips and blew so that the lock tender would know they were coming. When they approached the lock a short time later, he blew on it again. *Wo–o–o–o! Wo–o–o–o!*

Elias was surprised when a young woman with dark hair pulled into a loose bun at the back of her head, came out of the large stone house next to the canal and cranked open the lockgate. The last time he'd come through here with Grandpa, it had been an older man who'd opened the Walnutport lock. This petite woman didn't look strong enough to be doing such hard work. But maybe she was stronger than she appeared. Maybe her husband was sick or had business in town, and she was taking over for him today. Elias figured it wasn't his business to worry about whoever was tending the lock. As long it opened and his boat made it through, that's all that mattered.

Elias directed his gaze to Bobby, waiting off to one side with the mules. The boy had been working hard and trying his best, despite Ned's constant nagging.

Once the lock tender had opened the gates and Elias's boat had made it through, Ned called to Bobby, "Get the team movin'!"

The mules' ears twitched as they moved slowly forward.

Ned turned to Elias and smiled. "Can ya believe how easily that little lady handled the gates for us?"

Elias shook his head. "I was surprised to see a woman doing the job of a man."

"That was Sarah Turner," Ned said. "Her husband, Sam, died nearly a year ago, when he fell and got himself smashed between the lock and one of the boats. Sarah's been actin' as lock tender ever since, and with her havin' three kids to look after, I'm sure it ain't no easy task."

"No, I suppose not."

When another conch shell blew behind them, Elias glanced over his shoulder and saw Sarah Turner run out of her house to open the gate again. "She must be exhausted by the end of each day," he remarked.

Ned tugged on his beard, sprinkled with a bit of gray. "Only day off she gets is Sundays, when the canal closes down."

Elias knew the reason for that, and it made good sense to him. Besides the fact that Sunday was the Lord's Day, the rugged, hardworking canalers needed a day of rest, and he was sure that the lady lock tender needed one, too.

As they continued on their way, Elias found himself beginning to relax. He felt more at peace than he had in a very long time.

"I think I'm going to enjoy running this boat up and down the canal," he said to Ned, who'd pulled a piece of chewing tobacco from his shirt pocket.

"Are ya sure ya won't miss workin' in the office at your daddy's newspaper business?"

"I don't think so," Elias said with a shake of his head. "Running a newspaper is nothing like this—especially one in a busy town like Easton." The truth was, having his father scrutinize everything he did had made Elias feel insecure and inferior, like he could never measure up. He'd tried for a good many years to make Father proud, but all Father ever did was find fault. Well, maybe after Elias proved he could run this canal boat, Father would finally take notice and say a few kind words about Elias's accomplishment. Then again, by taking over Grandpa's boat, Elias may have ruined all chances of him and Father ever making peace.

Chapter 3

"*W*hat's wrong with the mules? Why aren't they moving?" Elias called over to his young driver.

"Don't know!" Bobby pushed a lock of sandy brown hair away from his face and grunted. "They was movin' just fine a few minutes ago." He motioned to Daisy and then Dolly. "All of a sudden, they both just stopped dead in their tracks."

"That's 'cause there's a huge puddle in the middle of the towpath," Ned said as he joined Elias at the bow of the boat. "Mules hate water, and Dolly and Daisy ain't no exception. They'll do anything to avoid walkin' through water—even a puddle."

"Oh yeah, that's right." Elias thumped the side of his head. He glanced over his shoulder. Another boat was coming up behind them. "What shall we do to get the mules moving?" he asked Ned.

"Gotta take 'em around the water." Ned leaned over the bow of the boat and shouted to Bobby, "Lead the mules around the puddle! Take 'em through the tall grass!"

"Haw!" Bobby shouted at the mules.

"Not *haw!*" Ned bellowed. "*Haw* means to the left. *Gee* means to the right!" He looked at Elias and groaned. "Ya should've hired a driver with more experience."

"Bobby was the only boy I could find on such short notice," Elias said. "Besides, the poor kid's folks are in need of money, and I thought I could help by giving him a job."

"Humph!" Ned snorted. "Then he'd better be a quick learner, or it'll take us a week instead of a few days to get up the canal to Mauch Chunk!"

Ignoring Ned's tirade, Elias turned his attention back to the mules. "Lead them to the right, Bobby. Lead them to the right!"

"Gee!" Bobby yelled.

When the mules didn't budge, he grabbed hold of their bridles and had just started moving them toward the thick grass when a deep voice hollered from behind Elias's boat, "Get outa my way; my boat's comin' through!"

"We can't do nothin' about movin' the boat to one side until that stupid boy gets them mules walkin' again," Ned muttered, shaking his head. He cupped his hands around his mouth and hollered at the other boat captain, "Just hold your boat back a minute, Bart, and we'll let ya pass!"

Elias was tempted to climb out of the boat and swim to shore so he could see if he might be able to help Bobby get Dolly and Daisy moving faster, but he quickly dismissed that dumb idea. It would be foolish to get his clothes wet for no good reason, because Bobby seemed to be managing okay. It was just taking much longer than Elias would have liked; especially with the burly, dark-haired fellow in the boat behind them, waving his hands and hollering, "Get that boat outa my way!"

If I'm gong to make it as a canal boat captain, I'll need to pay closer attention to things, Elias told himself. *And I'll have to try harder to remember more of what Grandpa taught me about running this boat.*

Sarah had just let another boat through the lock when she spotted her sister, Kelly, walking along the towpath next to the canal with her two children: Marcus, who was three, and Anna, who'd recently turned four.

As usual, Kelly's dark hair hung down her back in long, gentle waves. With the exception of Sundays, Kelly rarely wore her hair up in a bun.

"It's good to see you," Sarah said when Kelly and the children joined her on the section of towpath that ran along the front of the lock tender's house.

Kelly smiled. "It's good to see you, too. Except for our time together on Sundays, we don't get to see you as much as we'd like."

"I know. There's not much chance for me to get away." Sarah motioned to the lockgate. "With boats coming through at all hours, I'm needed here every day but Sunday."

"I'm sorry you have to work so hard." Kelly gave Sarah a hug. "I wish there was more I could do to help, but with two young ones to care for, helping Mike run the store, and trying to squeeze in time for painting, I don't have much free time on my hands these days."

"You can't sell any of your artwork if you don't take the time to paint."

"That's true, and I do love to paint. Have ever since I was a girl and could hold a piece of homemade charcoal in my hands." Kelly smiled. "I'm ever so grateful that Mike added on to the store so I could have my own little gallery where I can paint and sell my work."

Sarah nodded. "So what brings you over here today?"

"Things have been kind of slow at the store this morning, so I decided to take the kids outside for some fresh air and a walk." She glanced down at Marcus, who was now down on his knees inspecting a beetle. Anna stood beside him, her face lifted to the sun. "I thought maybe they could play with your kids awhile."

"Sammy's at school, of course, but Willis and Helen were playing on the porch awhile ago, when I was doing our laundry in the metal washtub," Sarah said. "When the last boat came through the lock, I sent them inside."

Kelly gave Sarah's shoulder a tender squeeze. "Are things going okay? Are you managing to keep up?"

"Everything's about the same, but there's always so much to do. Between tending the lock, washing clothes, and making bread to sell to the boatmen, I hardly have any time to spend with my kids." Sarah sighed deeply. "Seems like they're always trying to get my attention, and there's just not enough of me to go around."

"What about Maria? Isn't she keeping the kids occupied during the day?"

"Maria's not doing well. Her vision problem seems to be getting worse, and she's always so tired. It's all she can do to keep the house clean and help cook our meals, much less keep an eye on my two youngest all day."

Kelly's mouth formed an O. "Are you saying that Willis and Helen have been fending for themselves when you're out here tending the lock?"

"Maria does what she can to keep them occupied, but she's not up to caring for them the way I would if I could be with them all the time."

"Say, I have an idea," Kelly said. "Why don't I take Willis and Helen home with me for the rest of the day? That way they can play with Marcus and Anna. It'll give Maria a break, and you won't have to worry about them while you bake bread and tend the lock."

"Are you sure you don't mind? I mean, how are you going to help Mike in the store if you have four kids to keep an eye on all day?"

"I told you, things have been slow at the store today. Besides, Willis is old enough to keep the other three entertained if Mike needs me for anything. Since our house is connected to the store, if there's a problem, Willis can come and get me."

Sarah hesitated, but finally nodded. "You're right, Willis is always thinking up something to keep Helen entertained, and it would be a big help if Maria didn't have to be responsible for the kids today."

"Let's go inside and get them now," Kelly said. "Then the five of us will be on our way."

When Sarah, Kelly, and Kelly's children entered the house, Sarah was surprised to see her six-year-old son and four-year-old daughter sitting in the middle of the kitchen floor with a bag of flour between them. They'd scooped some of it onto the floor, some into a baking pan, and a good deal of it was in Helen's dark hair.

"What in the world are you two doing?" Sarah asked, squatting down beside them.

"We're makin' bread." Helen smiled up at Sarah, and swiped a floury hand across her turned-up nose. "It was Willis's idea."

"Where's your grandma?" Sarah asked. Surely Maria wouldn't have let the kids make a mess like this if she'd known what they were doing.

"Grandma's in there." Willis pointed to the door leading to their small, but cozy, parlor. Sarah noticed then that he had some flour in his light brown hair as well. So much for Willis keeping Helen entertained.

25

"I'll clean up this mess while you talk to Maria," Kelly offered.

"Thanks, I appreciate that." Sarah rose to her feet and hurried from the room.

When she entered the parlor she gasped. There lay Maria, facedown on the floor!

Chapter 4

"*W*ell, wouldn't ya just know it?" Ned shouted from where he'd been stirring a pot of bean soup sitting on the small, coal-burning cookstove in the middle of the boat. For some reason, Ned preferred cooking on it rather than the slightly larger stove that was below in the galley.

Elias, not wanting to take his eyes off the waterway ahead, glanced quickly over his shoulder. "What's wrong, Ned?"

"We're outa bread. Shouldn't have ate any at breakfast, I guess."

"That's okay. We can do without bread for lunch."

"Maybe so, but we'll need it tomorrow, and the next day, too."

"We can stop at one of the stores between here and Easton and pick up a loaf of bread."

"Stoppin' at a store would take too long. We'd end up lookin' at other things we don't really need, and there's no time for lollygaggin' today." Ned pulled a hunk of chewing tobacco from his shirt pocket and popped into his mouth. "Already spent too much time up in Mauch Chunk, waitin' on the other boats that was ahead of us. When that noisy, sooty train showed up, it took a load of coal before we even got up to the loadin' chute."

"You're right, it did take a long time to get our coal." Elias hoped it wouldn't be that way every time they went to Mauch Chunk, but if it was, they'd just have to deal with it.

"Guess we could always see if that lady lock tender in Walnutport has any bread we could buy," Ned suggested. "She often sells bread to the boatmen who come through her lock."

"Sure, we can do that."

They traveled in silence for a while, interrupted only by the sound of the water lapping against the boat and an occasional undignified grunt from Ned as he stirred the soup on the stove.

"Here's a cup of soup for ya, boss," Ned said, stepping up to Elias a short time later.

Elias took the warm cup in his hands. "Thanks."

"Got any idea what you'll do once the railroad takes over haulin' all the coal in these here parts?" Ned asked, leaning against the side of the boat.

"I'm not sure. To be honest, I haven't really thought about it that much."

"Well you'd better think about it, 'cause it's bound to happen sooner or later."

"I guess I'll deal with that when it comes. I'm just taking one day at a time right now."

"If the time comes that you can't boat any longer, will ya go back to work at your daddy's newspaper office?"

Elias shook his head. "That will never happen. My father's not even speaking to me right now."

"How come?"

"He thinks I was foolish for leaving the newspaper and taking over Grandpa's boat. The way he talks about the poor man, you'd never know Grandpa was his father." Elias frowned. "Father said if I left Easton to captain Grandpa's boat I'd never work for him again."

Ned leaned his head over the boat and spit out his wad of tobacco. "Aw, I'm sure he didn't mean it. Probably just said that, hopin' you'd change your mind. If you was to leave the canal and return to Easton, he'd probably welcome ya back with open arms."

"I'm not so sure about that." Elias shrugged. "But I'm not going to worry about it either. I'm just going to do the job Grandpa wanted me to do."

"Guess that's the best way to deal with things all right." Ned pointed up ahead. "Looks like Walnutport's comin' into view. You'd best get out the conch shell and let the lock tender know that you're needin' to come through."

"Maria! Maria, can you hear me?" Sarah's heart pounded as she knelt on the floor beside her pale-faced mother-in-law.

Kelly entered the room just then and gasped. "Oh my! Is . . . is she dead?"

"No, thank goodness. I can see by the rise and fall of her chest that she's breathing." Sarah cradled Maria's head in her hands. "I think we should get Dr. McGrath."

Kelly stood. "I'll run into town and see if he's at his office. If he's there, I'll ask if he can come look at Maria right away."

Just then, Maria's eyes fluttered open, but she stared at Sarah with a blank expression. "Wh–what's going on? What am I doin' on the floor?"

"Kelly and I were outside visiting, and when I came into the parlor, I found you lying here."

"What happened, Maria? Did you get dizzy and pass out?" Kelly questioned.

"I . . . uh . . . was heading upstairs to do some cleaning, and all of a sudden everything looked real blurry. Guess I must have tripped on the braided throw rug. Then I lost my balance, and . . ." She rubbed her forehead. "I must've hit my head, and then everything went dark."

"Let's get you over to the sofa so you can rest," Sarah said. "Then Kelly's going into town to get the doctor."

"There's no need for that." Maria pushed herself to a sitting position. "Once I get my bearings, I'll be fine."

"You're not fine, Maria. You fell and hit your

head. Now I insist that you lie down awhile," Sarah said.

"Oh, all right."

Sarah took hold of Maria's left arm, and Kelly took her right arm; then they guided her to the sofa. They'd no more than gotten her settled when a knock sounded on the door.

"I'll see who that is." Kelly hurried from the room.

When she returned, young Pastor William and his wife, Betsy, were with her.

"We were taking a walk along the towpath and thought we'd stop in to visit and see how things are going here." Betsy smiled at Sarah, but her bright eyes and cheerful expression quickly turned to a look of concern when she saw Maria on the sofa. "What's wrong? Is Maria sick?"

Sarah quickly explained what had happened. "Maria's vision seems to be getting worse, but she refuses to see Dr. McGrath," she said, hoping Pastor William or Betsy might intervene. "I've suggested that Maria move back to Easton to live with her son, but she's flatly refused."

"Sarah's right." Pastor William moved over to the sofa and took Maria's hand. "The last time I was here, you were having trouble seeing, and I think you ought to see the doctor today and tell him what's happened," he said in his usual gentle tone.

Maria shook her head stubbornly. "I'll be fine; I just need to rest awhile."

"When Dr. McGrath examined Maria's eyes a few weeks ago, he said her vision's getting worse," Sarah said.

Betsy's pale blond hair, which she'd worn down, swished across her shoulder as she knelt on the floor in front of where Maria sat. "If you moved back to Easton, you'd have access to a hospital and many good doctors, and you'd be cared for in your son's house and wouldn't have the responsibility for caring for Sarah's three active children."

Tears welled in Maria's eyes. "I . . . I love those kids, and I couldn't move away and leave Sarah alone with no one to watch them. Who would take care of things while she's outside tending the lock?"

"I'll manage somehow," Sarah said with a catch in her voice.

"Maybe I can come over to help out when things aren't real busy at the store," Kelly volunteered.

"Better yet, I can come over here to help out." Betsy looked at Maria. "Would you be willing to move back to Easton if I did that?"

Before Maria could reply, the low moan of a conch shell floated through the door that Kelly had left open.

Sarah stood. "A boat's coming through, and I need to go out and open the lock. We'll have to finish this discussion when I come back."

Chapter 5

As soon as Sarah ran out the front door, she realized there was more than one boat waiting to come through the lock. In fact, there were three.

"Oh great," she moaned. "It'll take me forever to get back inside."

Lifting the edge of her long gray skirt, she hurried to open the first set of gates. Once the boat was completely in, she closed the gates and opened the wickets in the lower set of gates so that water flowed out of the lock, allowing the boat to drop slowly. Then the next set of gates was opened, allowing the mules to pull the boat on down the canal.

As the second boat came through the lock, Sarah's face contorted. The captain of the boat was Bart Jarmon, a tall burly man with thick black hair and a full, wooly-looking beard to match. Bart's foul mouth and overbearing ways were bad enough to deal with, but ever since Sam had died, Bart had often made suggestive remarks whenever he saw Sarah. Once, he'd even been so bold as to suggest that the two of them should get hitched, saying she could quit her job as lock tender and spend her days on his boat, cooking, cleaning, and washing his dirty clothes.

This canal would have to freeze over solid in the middle of summer before I'd ever consider marrying someone like Bart. Sarah gritted her teeth. *And what kind of stepfather would he make for my kids?*

She thought about the time, before Betsy married Pastor William, when Bart had gone to Betsy's place to pick up some clothes she'd washed for him. She could still see the look of disgust on Betsy's face when she'd later confided that after Bart had boldly kissed her, she'd thrown his wet shirt at him and told him never to come back.

Bart would be a lot wetter than he was then if he tried something like that with me, Sarah thought. *I'd push him into the muddy canal if he even looked like he was going to kiss me!*

Much to Sarah's relief, Bart wasn't steering the boat. His helper, Clem Smith, an elderly man with several missing teeth, was at the tiller. Sarah figured Bart was probably below on his bunk, sleeping off the effects from the whiskey he'd likely had the night before.

Sarah exchanged only a few words with Clem and kept her mind on the business at hand. She knew how dangerous it could be for a lock tender who didn't pay close attention to what they were doing. Some lock tenders had gotten knocked over when they tried to get the pin in the wicket with one hand while they cranked with the other. If Sarah said more than a few words to any of the boatmen, it was usually after she'd finished the dangerous details of opening and closing the lock.

After Bart's boat passed through the lock, the next one came in, steered by Elias Brooks, the new boatman Sarah had met on his last trip through.

"My helper said you might have some bread to sell," Elias called to her.

She gave a quick nod. "There's some in the house."

"I'd like to buy a couple of loaves if you have any to spare." Elias pulled his fingers through his thick reddish-blond hair, cut just below his ears.

Sarah noticed for the first time that he had a large red blotch on his left cheek. No doubt, he'd been born with it.

She pulled her gaze quickly away for fear that he would think she'd been staring at him. "I'll get the bread as soon as your boat goes through. If you have time, you can tie up to one of the posts along the bank."

Elias looked at Ned, as though seeking his approval. Ned turned his hands palms up. "Guess we'll have to 'cause we do need the bread."

"That's what we'll do," Elias said with a nod.

Sarah did her job, and after Elias's boat made it through the lock, he maneuvered the boat toward the bank, while she hurried to the house to get the bread.

When she stepped inside, she stuck her head into the parlor. Maria was still on the sofa, and Kelly and Betsy sat in the chairs across from her.

"Where's Pastor William?" Sarah asked.

"He went to get Dr. McGrath," Betsy replied.

Sarah had been so busy with the boats that she hadn't seen the pastor leave her house.

"I need to take some bread to one of the boatmen," she said. "I'll be back as soon as I can."

Kelly smiled. "No problem. Take your time."

Sarah rushed into the kitchen, grabbed two loaves of bread, and ran out the door. She was halfway up the wooden plank leading to Elias's boat when her foot caught on a loose board, and one of the loaves flew out of her hands. She lunged for it, and gasped when it plopped into the canal.

Elias raced down the ramp and grabbed Sarah's arm. "Are you okay?"

Sarah's face heated as she nodded slowly. She felt like a clumsy fool. "I–I'm so sorry, but I dropped one of your loaves of bread into the canal."

Quack! Quack! Quack! A pair of mallard ducks landed on the water and quickly converged on the bread.

"Well, at least it won't go to waste," Elias said with a chuckle.

Sarah handed him the one good loaf. "I'll go back to the house and get you another."

"I'll walk with you," Elias said. "That way you won't have to come back out here again."

"At least not until another boat comes," Sarah

35

muttered. This had not been a good way to begin her day.

Elias waited on the porch while Sarah went into the house. When she entered the kitchen to get another loaf of bread, Bristle Face, the scruffy-looking terrier Betsy had given them several months ago, ran in front of her, and she nearly lost her balance.

Sarah looked at Willis, who sat at the kitchen table with Helen and their cousins. "Would you please hold on to the dog until I've gone back outside?"

"Sure, Mama."

Sarah stuck her head into the parlor again. "Is everything okay in here?"

"Maria's sleeping," Betsy whispered. "Are you done outside?"

"Not yet. I accidentally dropped a loaf of bread into the canal and had to get a new one."

"Is there anything I can do to help?" Kelly asked.

"I think everything's under control. Elias Brooks is waiting outside for his bread, and he was very nice about the bread I dropped. I'll just be a few more minutes."

Sarah hurried outside, and found Elias sitting on the porch step, talking with his young mule driver, as well as Sammy, who'd just gotten home from school.

"Do you get to do much fishing in the canal?" Elias asked Sammy.

Sammy shook his head. "Used to fish some when Papa was alive." He glanced up at Sarah. "Mama's too busy for fishin', and she won't let me fish alone."

"Sure wish I had time to go fishin'." Bobby stared at the canal with a wistful expression. "But I guess that's never gonna happen 'cause I'm too busy leadin' the mules."

"Maybe some Sunday we can do some fishing," Elias said.

Bobby's eyes lit up, and so did Sammy's. "Ya mean it?" Bobby asked.

Elias nodded. "Sure thing."

"Can I fish with ya?" Sammy asked.

"If we're anywhere near here on a Sunday, we'd be happy to have you join us. That is, if your mother doesn't mind." Elias looked up at Sarah, as if to gauge her response.

"I—I don't know." Sarah leaned on the porch railing. She became edgy any time her children got too close to the water. After Sam had been killed, she'd been more nervous than ever.

Sammy tugged on the edge of Sarah's apron. "Please, Mama. Can I go fishin' with Bobby and the nice man?"

Not wishing to create a scene or embarrass Sammy, Sarah patted the top of his head and said, "We'll have to wait and see how it goes." Secretly, she hoped that Elias never stopped anywhere near Walnutport on a Sunday.

Chapter 6

*A*s Sarah, followed by Sammy, approached their front door, Pastor William showed up with the doctor.

"I'm so glad you're here, Dr. McGrath. As you know, Maria hasn't been feeling well for some time. Earlier today, she fell and hit her head because she couldn't see where she was going." Sarah drew in a quick breath. "I'm really worried about her, and we've been trying to talk her into moving to Easton to live with her son, Roger, but she refuses to go."

Dr. McGrath nodded his nearly bald head. "Pastor William has already filled me in. So let's go inside, and after I've examined Maria, I'll see if I can convince her to move."

"I appreciate that."

As Dr. McGrath and Pastor William headed for the parlor, Sarah ushered Sammy into the kitchen where the other children were playing.

"Is . . . is Grandma gonna die, Mama?" Sammy's chin trembled, and his blue eyes widened.

"No, son, but she's losing her eyesight, and it's not good for her to be here anymore. She needs to be in Easton where she can get help for her eyes and have someone to take care of her."

"I'll take care of her, and I'll keep an eye on Helen and Willis, too. I can quit school and stay home so

I can help with whatever you need to have done."

Sarah gave Sammy's shoulder a gentle squeeze. "It's nice of you to volunteer, but you're still a little boy. Taking care of Grandma would be a full-time job, not to mention your busy little brother and sister." She tweaked the end of his nose. "Besides, you need to go to school so you can learn to read and write. You need to get an education so you can get a good-paying job when you grow up—something that will get you away from the canal."

Deep wrinkles etched his small forehead. "But I like the canal. Just wish I could go fishin' whenever I wanted to."

"Maybe your uncle Mike will take you fishing sometime, but you're never to go near the water when you're alone. Is that clear?"

He nodded. "That nice man with the red blotch on his face said he'd take me fishin' some Sunday. Can I go with him, Mama? Can I, please?"

"We go to church on Sundays; you know that."

"How 'bout after church? That canaler said some Sunday afternoon, so he must've meant after church."

"We'll see, Sammy. In the meantime, I want you to go in the kitchen." Sarah opened the door. "Now, shoo."

"Here you go," Elias said, handing the bread he'd bought to Ned. "This should last us for a few days, don't you think?"

Ned grunted. "I s'pose it will, but after all the time you spent gabbin' to the lock tender, we'll be even later gettin' to Easton with our load of coal."

"We'll get there when we get there."

Ned glanced over his shoulder. "Sure is a shame a purty lady like Sarah has to work so hard to provide for her kids."

Elias nodded. "Here on the canal, a lot of men and women work hard for a living."

"Which is why I can't figure out how come a smart, school-learned man like yourself would wanna run this here boat."

"I've told you before . . . I'm honoring my grandfather's wishes." Elias motioned to the trees bordering the towpath along the canal. "Besides, I enjoy it here on the water. It's peaceful, and the folks who live along here are down-to-earth, not phony."

"It ain't always so peaceful," Ned said with a shake of his head. "When some liquored-up canaler starts spoutin' off at some other fella, things can get real loud and ugly 'round here. Not to mention some of the brawls that take place when someone loses his temper 'cause they're tryin' to beat some other boat through the lock." Ned cupped his hands around his mouth and turned away from Elias. "Hey, mule boy," he called to Bobby, "quit draggin' your feet and get them mules movin' faster! We ain't got all day, ya know!"

Elias's jaw clenched as he ground his teeth together. Why did Ned think he needed to shout orders at Bobby like that? This was Elias's boat, and he was the only one who should be giving orders.

Of course, he reasoned, *the boy was walking kind of slow and probably did need a bit of prodding. It just could have been done in a nicer tone.*

"I don't think you need to holler at Bobby like that," Elias told Ned. "A little kindness goes a long way, you know."

Ned slapped the side of his pant leg and snorted real loud. "A little kindness might go a long way if you're tryin' to court some purty woman, but ya need to let your mule driver know who's boss from the get-go, or he'll slow ya down. And that'll cost ya more money than he's worth."

"I'll take your advice under consideration."

When Sarah stepped into the parlor, she stood off to one side with the others as Dr. McGrath examined Maria. When he was done, he took Maria's hand and said, "Your eyes have gotten much worse, and as I've said before, without proper treatment it's only a matter of time before you'll be completely blind. I do think you'd be better off in Easton, where you can be seen by a specialist."

Maria opened her mouth as if to respond, but

Sarah cut her off. "I'm going to send Roger a letter tomorrow morning and ask him to come get you."

Betsy stepped forward. "And you don't need to worry about anything here, because we'll see that Sarah gets all the help she needs."

Tears welled in Maria's eyes as she slowly nodded. "I'll go, but I don't have to like it."

Sarah knew she and the children would miss Maria, but it was for the best. She just wished she didn't have to rely on Betsy and Kelly for help, because they both had busy lives of their own. If only there was some other kind of work she could do to support her children. She just didn't know what it could be.

Chapter 7

*O*ne week later, Roger came to escort Maria to Easton.

As Sarah helped Maria pack her bags, she was filled with a deep sense of sadness. It was hard to let Maria go. The dear woman had lived with them after Sarah and Sam came back to the canal when Sammy was still a little guy. Then when Sam's father died, Maria had gone to live with Roger and his wife in Easton, but she'd returned to the canal to help Sarah after Sam was killed. Sarah had become dependent on Maria, and the children were attached to her, too.

"I wish I didn't have to go," Maria said. "I wish my eyes weren't failing me."

Sarah took a seat on the bed beside Maria and slipped her arm around Maria's waist. "I wish that, too, and we're going to miss you very much, but moving to Easton is the best thing for you right now."

Maria sighed. "I know."

A knock sounded on the bedroom door. "Are you ready, Mom? We need to get a move on if we're going to catch our train to Easton," Roger called through the closed door.

"Come in," Sarah said. She closed Maria's reticule and set it on the floor.

"Is everything ready?" Roger asked as he entered the room.

"Yes, her trunk is packed, and so is her smaller reticule." Sarah swallowed past the lump in her throat. Roger, though a bit taller and a few years older than Sam, looked so much like him. Roger had the same blond hair and blue eyes as his brother, only Roger sported a handlebar mustache, and Sam had always been clean-shaven. Roger worked at Glendon Iron Works, not far from Easton, and his wife, Mary, who was home all day, would be the one responsible for taking care of Maria. Sarah found comfort in knowing that Maria would have good care in Easton.

Sarah picked up the reticule, and Roger lifted Maria's trunk. Then they all went downstairs. The children, who'd been eating breakfast in the kitchen, gathered around Maria near the door.

"Sure wish you didn't hafta go," Sammy said, his voice quivering as he struggled not to cry.

Maria patted the top of his head. "Maybe you can come to Easton to visit me sometime."

"That ain't never gonna happen," Sammy said with a shake of his head. "Mama has to be here all the time so she can open the lock."

"Maybe you can visit us sometime this winter when the canal's closed," Roger suggested.

Sarah bit her lip to keep from saying what was on her mind. With her limited funds, she didn't see any way that they'd ever be able to afford a trip to Easton. She wasn't about to tell Sammy that, though. No point in upsetting him any more than he already was.

"Well, it's time to go," Roger said. "If we don't head out now, we will miss our train."

Maria bent to give each of the children a hug, then she turned to Sarah and said, "Take care. I'll be praying for you."

Sarah hugged Maria. "I'll be praying for you, too."

When Betsy arrived at Sarah's, she found Sarah outside, letting a boat through the lock. "Oh no," she muttered. "I should have gotten here sooner. I'm sure the children are in the house by themselves, and poor Sarah must be worried about them."

Betsy hurried to the house, where she found Sarah's children sitting at the kitchen table, coloring a picture. "I thought you would have left for school by now," she said to Sammy.

He shook his head. "Since there was no one here to watch Willis and Helen, Mama said I should stay until you got here, 'cause someone has to keep an eye on 'em."

"I'm so sorry. I should have been here sooner." Betsy pulled out a chair and took a seat beside Sammy. "Now that I'm here, you can go to school."

His nose crinkled as he frowned. "I'd rather stay here so I can teach Bristle Face some new tricks. I wanna teach him to play dead and roll over."

"You can do that after you get home from school."

His eyes brightened. "Since Bristle Face used to be your dog, do ya wanna help me teach him some tricks?"

"I probably won't be here when you get home from school," Betsy said. "Your aunt Kelly will be taking over for me later this afternoon so I can practice the songs I'll be playing this Sunday at church." She smiled at the children. "If your mother's willing, I'd like to have you all over to our house for lunch after church lets out."

"Oh, Mama will be willing," Sammy said. "Now that Grandma's gone, Mama will be stuck with all the cookin' whether she likes it or not."

Betsy suppressed a smile. Children could be so honest about things. She looked forward to the day that she and William would have children of their own. Of course, they'd only been married since Christmas of last year, so most folks would say they still had plenty of time. Betsy didn't see it that way, though. She was thirty-three and wanted some children before she was too old to enjoy them.

She pointed to Sammy's lunch pail sitting on the counter. "You'd better head to school now, Sammy, or you'll really be late."

He grunted as he pushed his chair aside and stood. "Okay. I'll see ya tomorrow, Betsy."

"Hey, mule boy, get a move on!" Ned shouted from the bow of the boat. "How come you're draggin' your feet again?"

"I ain't feelin' so well," Bobby called in return. "Think I might throw up."

Ned flapped his hand, like he was shooing away a pesky fly. "Aw, quit your bellyachin' and get a move on now!"

Elias frowned as he stepped up to Ned. "Stop yelling at the boy. If he's sick, then we can't make him work."

Ned's forehead wrinkled, and he popped a piece of chewing tobacco in his mouth. "If that boy don't keep walkin', we'll never get this load of coal back to Easton."

"But if he's sick . . ."

"He ain't sick. He's just lazy, that's all."

Elias shook his head. "I don't think he's lazy. I think . . ."

"What in tarnation is that boy doin'?" Ned leaned over the boat and shook his fist. "What are ya doin' there in the bushes?"

Bobby, who was now crouched behind a clump of bushes, rose slowly to his feet as he clutched his stomach. "Just lost my breakfast, and I feel kinda weak."

"That's it, we're stopping!" Elias grabbed the tiller and turned the boat into the bank.

"What are we stoppin' for?" Ned grumbled. "We'll never get to Easton if we stop here."

"Bobby's too sick to lead the mules," Elias said. "He needs to lie on his bunk and rest, because if he keeps walking, he'll probably keel over."

Ned grunted. "What are you plannin' to do? Are ya goin' to leave the boat here until the boy feels well enough to walk?"

"No, I'll lead the mules, and you can steer the boat."

Ned's bushy eyebrows shot straight up. "Are you kiddin' me?"

"No, I'm certainly not. If we want to keep going, then it's the only thing we can do."

Ned spit his wad of chewing tobacco into the canal. "That's great. Just great! I doubt that you can lead the mules any better than the kid."

Elias set his lips in a firm line. He'd show Ned how well he could lead the mules.

Chapter 8

*T*he next morning as Sarah was about to join her children for breakfast, she heard the familiar moaning of a conch shell.

"Oh no," she said with a groan. "Another boat's coming through." She'd begun working at five thirty and had already opened the lock to six boats.

The conch shell blew again, and Sarah knew that even though Betsy hadn't arrived yet, she really must go.

"Sammy, keep an eye on your sister and brother," she instructed.

"Okay, Mama."

"And don't any of you leave the house," she said as she hurried out the door.

Sarah's fingers felt stiff and cold as she struggled to put the pin in the wicket.

Suddenly, before Sarah realized what had happened, she was jerked backward and fell on her back. A stab of pain shot through her ribs. She was sure they must be broken. She tried to sit up, but the pain was so intense, all she could do was lie there and moan.

Elias had been walking the towpath since yesterday morning, and he was beginning to have an appreciation for how hard young Bobby worked.

The boy was feeling somewhat better today, but was still too weak to walk. So Elias had decided to lead the mules again, as he was determined to see that Bobby got the rest he needed.

As Elias approached the Walnutport lock, he was shocked when he saw Sarah Turner get knocked to the ground.

"We need to stop!" he hollered at Ned.

"What for?" Ned leaned over the boat and glared at Elias. "I thought we was supposed to be goin' through the lock."

"The lock tender's been hurt!" Elias pointed to where Sarah lay on the ground. "I'm going over there to check on her." He secured the mules' lead rope to a nearby post and dashed over to where Sarah lay.

"What happened? Are you hurt?" he asked, squatting down beside her.

"I . . . I was pulling the pin from the wicket and ended up flat on my back." She curled her fingers into the palms of her hands tightly, obviously trying not to cry. "I think I may have broken my ribs."

"Let me help you into the house, and then I'll go into town and get the doctor," he said.

She shook her head. "I can't go in the house. Someone has to let your boat through the lock."

"I'll have Ned secure my boat, and then he can tend to the lock if any other boats should come through."

"Oh no, I couldn't expect him to do that. I need to—" She flinched as she tried to stand.

"You're in no shape to be working right now. I'm taking you into the house." Gently, Elias slipped his arm around Sarah's waist, and then he walked her slowly toward the house. They were almost there when Betsy Covington, the preacher's wife whom he'd met at Cooper's store the last time he'd stopped, showed up. When she looked at Sarah, her face registered immediate concern.

"Sarah, what happened?"

Sarah explained what had happened to her, and then Elias told Betsy that Ned was going to take care of the lock while he went to fetch the doctor.

"That's so nice of you," Betsy said. "Let's get Sarah inside so she can lie down."

They stepped into the house, and Elias helped Sarah into the parlor and over to the sofa. "I'm going out to tell Ned what he needs to do, and then I'll head to the doctor's office." He paused and looked at Betsy. "I'm not that familiar with Walnutport yet. Where is the doctor's office anyway?"

"It's on Main Street, next to the barber shop."

"Thanks." Elias turned and hurried out the door.

When he stepped outside, he found Ned standing by the post where he'd tied the mules.

"Sarah may have broken some ribs, so you're going to have to act as lock tender while I get the doctor," Elias said.

Ned's bushy eyebrows furrowed. "You've gotta be kidding!"

"You told me once that you'd worked as a lock tender for a while."

Ned shrugged. "So?"

"So I'm sure you know exactly what to do."

Ned motioned to the boat, which he'd tied up. "What about our load? How are we gonna get that delivered to Easton if we waste time hangin' around here?"

Elias's spine stiffened. "Helping someone in need is not a waste of time. And for your information, I'm wasting time right now, standing here arguing with you when I should be on my way to the doctor's office."

Ned grunted. "You're a do-gooder, just like your grandpappy was."

Elias smiled. He saw being compared to his grandfather as a compliment. "Are you going to tend the lock or not?" he asked Ned.

Ned released a noisy grunt. "I'll do whatever you say, but only because you're the boss."

Chapter 9

*W*hen Elias returned with Dr. McGrath, Pastor William was at the house. "How's Sarah doing?" he asked Betsy, who sat at the kitchen table with the children.

"I fixed her some tea, and she's resting on the

sofa, but every time another conch shell blows, she gets upset and says it's not right for someone else to be doing her job." Betsy rose from her seat and came to stand beside him. "I'm really concerned about her. She pushes herself too hard and is doing the work of a man when I'm sure she'd rather be taking care of her children."

"Sarah needs to provide for them," Pastor William said. "And she's been doing a good job of it, wouldn't you say?"

Betsy nodded. "But now that she's been hurt, she may not be able to work at all."

"Ned's helping out," Elias interjected.

"That's true, but he can't tend the lock indefinitely," Betsy said.

Pastor William slipped his arm around Betsy's waist. "Let's wait and see what the doctor says. In the meantime, the best thing we can do for Sarah is to pray."

"Well, your ribs don't appear to be broken," Dr. McGrath said as he examined Sarah. "However, they are severely bruised. I'll give you some liniment to put on them, but you'll need to rest for the next few days to give your ribs a chance to heal so you don't injure them any further."

Sarah shook her head. "I can't lie around here and rest. I need to tend the lock."

"I'll be right back."

When Dr. McGrath left the parlor, Sarah leaned her head against the arm of the sofa and listened to the wood crackling in the fireplace. If not for the pain in her ribs it would have felt nice to lie here and relax.

A few minutes later, the doctor returned with Betsy, Pastor William, and Elias.

"The doctor told us that he wants you to rest, and I think I have an answer to your problem," Elias said as he approached the sofa.

Sarah tipped her head. "What's that?"

"My mule driver's sick right now, but if I can find someone to fill in for him, then I'll leave Ned here to tend the lock and I'll head to Easton with my load of coal. By the time I get back, you may feel up to tending the lock again."

"I'll lead the mules for you," Sammy said, rushing into the room.

Sarah shook her head vigorously. "Absolutely not! I won't have any child of mine walking the towpath for hours on end."

"We'll go slow and easy," Elias said. "And I'll make sure to keep a close eye on the boy."

Sammy took a seat on the sofa beside Sarah and clutched her hand. "Please, Mama. I know I can do it. It'll make me happy to do somethin' helpful while you're here gettin' better."

Sarah looked up at Pastor William, whose deep blue eyes wore a look of concern. "Will you please tell my son what a bad idea that is?"

"I can do it, Mama," Sammy said before the pastor could respond. "I'm good with animals, and I've walked the mules a bit when some of the boats have stopped at Uncle Mike's store."

Sarah frowned. "What were you doing walking the mules?"

"Wanted to see what it was like, so one of the mule drivers let me try it awhile." Sammy puffed out his chest. "Leadin' the mules wasn't hard a'tall. Fact is, I kinda liked it."

Sarah shook her head again. "I said no, and that's final."

"But, Mama . . ."

Holding her sides, Sarah gritted her teeth and pulled herself off the sofa. "I'm not seriously hurt, and there's no need for Ned to stay and tend the lock."

Betsy rushed forward and took Sarah's arm. "You heard what the doctor said. You're not up to working yet."

Pastor William nodded. "My wife is right. You need to spend a few days resting so your ribs can heal." He turned to Elias. "If your offer's still open to leave Ned here to tend the lock, then I'll head back to town and see if I can find a mule driver for you."

Elias nodded. "My offer's still open. I'll go explain the situation to Ned, and then I'll move my boat over to Cooper's store, because I need to get some supplies."

"Want me to lead the mules so ya can get the boat over to the store?" Sammy asked.

Sarah held up her hand. "No! You need to go to school."

"But I'm already late, Mama. Can't I stay home today and help out around here?"

"Betsy came here to help. Now I want you to head for school right now."

Sammy frowned. "Don't see why ya hafta treat me like a baby all the time. Don't see why ya don't want my help."

"It's not that I don't want your help. I just don't think you should miss any school." She motioned to the kitchen. "Now go get the lunch I made for you earlier and be on your way."

With shoulders hunched and head down, Sammy shuffled out the door.

Pastor William gave Betsy's shoulder a squeeze. "I'm off to see if I can round up a mule driver for Elias, and then there are a few members from our congregation I need to call on. I'll see you at home this evening."

Betsy smiled. "Have a good day."

Elias looked over at Sarah. "When I go to the store for supplies, I'll ask Mike Cooper if it'll be okay for Ned to bed down in his stable when he's done working for the day. But he'll be back over here early tomorrow morning, ready to tend the lock."

Sarah managed a weak smile. "Thank you, I appreciate that."

After Elias and William left, Betsy turned to Sarah and said, "I'm going out to the kitchen to check on the children, and then I'll make us a pot of hot tea. While I'm doing that, why don't you lie down and rest?"

Sarah heaved a sigh. "Oh, alright. I can see with you all ganging up on me that I really have no other choice."

"I still don't see why I have to hang around here playin' lock tender while you head to Easton," Ned said after Elias had instructed him to lead the mules so he could pull the boat over to Cooper's store.

"I told you already. Sarah's ribs are badly bruised, and the doctor wants her to rest."

"But how are you gonna manage on the boat without me, and who are you gonna get to lead the mules?"

"I've seen a few other canalers manage their boats alone, so I'll get by somehow." Elias pointed in the direction of town. "The pastor's gone looking for someone to lead the mules, and as soon as he shows up, I'll be on my way."

Ned folded his arms and spat on the ground. "This is somethin' like your grandpappy would've done, and all I've gotta say is, sometimes a body can be too nice!"

Elias shook his head. "There's no such thing as being too nice. It's a Christian's duty to—"

"Now don't start preachin' to me. I had enough of that when I was workin' for your grand-pappy."

"I'm not preaching. I'm only saying—"

"Don't care about a Christian's duty. I ain't no Christian, so my only duty is to work hard and try to earn a decent living."

Elias was tempted to argue, but he knew it would fall on deaf ears. He figured the best way to witness to Ned was through his actions. Maybe if he saw Christianity put into practice often enough, he'd realize he was missing something and would eventually seek the Lord.

"I'm getting back on the boat now," Elias said. "So it might be a good idea for you to get the mules heading down the towpath in the direction of the store before another boat comes along needing to get through the lock."

Ned grunted. "Whatever you say, boss."

Elias boarded the boat and took hold of the tiller. When they arrived in front of the store, he lowered the wooden plank and stepped onto the grassy bank. "You'd better get back to the lock now," he told Ned. "I hear a conch shell blowing in the distance, so it won't be long until the lock needs to be raised."

Ned opened his mouth like he might argue, but then he snapped it shut and ambled down the towpath in the direction of Sarah's house.

Elias hurried into the store, rounded up the

supplies he needed, and was about to pay for them when Sammy entered the store.

"What are you doing here?" Elias asked. "I thought you'd gone to school."

Sammy shook his head. "Went home to ask Mama one more time if I could lead your mules." He gave Elias a lopsided grin. "She finally gave in and said I could go."

Elias rubbed his chin as he studied the boy. "Are you sure about that?"

Sammy nodded. "Guess we'd better get goin', huh, mister . . . What's your name, anyway?"

"It's Elias. Elias Brooks." Elias looked at Mike Cooper, who stood behind the counter, boxing up his supplies. "If Pastor William comes by with someone to lead my mules, would you tell him I've already found a mule driver and that we're on our way to Easton?"

Mike's mustache twitched, and his forehead wrinkled as he studied Sammy. "Are you sure your mama said you could go with Elias?"

Sammy bobbed his head. "And I'm ready to go now!"

Mike looked back at Elias. "I personally think Sammy's too young to be leading the mules, but if Sarah said it was okay then I guess I have no say in it."

"Will you give Pastor William my message?" Elias asked.

Mike nodded. "I'll be sure to tell him."

Elias paid Mike, scooped up the box, and headed out the door behind Sammy. He hoped he wasn't making a mistake by taking the boy along, but the eager look on Sammy's face gave him the confidence to believe that everything would go just fine on the trip to Easton.

Chapter 10

Sarah yawned and pulled herself to a sitting position. She had no idea how long she'd been sleeping, but the shadows on her bedroom wall told her it must be late afternoon. She rose slowly from the bed and ambled over to the window facing the canal. A boat was going through the locks. She'd been sleeping so hard she hadn't even heard the captain blow his conch shell. As much as she hated to admit it, having Ned here to tend the lock was a comfort. It would have been difficult, maybe even impossible for her to carry out her duties, hurting the way she did.

Sarah's stomach growled, reminding her that she hadn't eaten anything since noon. It was probably getting close to supper, and the children would no doubt be hungry. She really should go downstairs and help get their supper going so Betsy could go home and fix something to eat for her and Pastor William.

Sarah moved over to the dresser and peered at herself in the oval looking glass. She'd taken her hair down when she'd come upstairs to rest, and it was a tangled mess. She squinted at her reflection as she pulled her comb through the ends of her hair. The dark circles lying beneath her eyes seemed more pronounced than usual.

Many days, the first boat would come through the lock as early as five in the morning, and the last boat might not arrive until nine thirty at night. The only day Sarah got to sleep in was Sunday. Even then, she was up early so she and the children could go to church. Sometimes Kelly would take Sarah's children to her house after church so Sarah could rest. She didn't know what she would do without the help of her sister, as well as her dear friend Betsy. Even near-strangers like Elias had offered help. She still couldn't believe that he'd headed to Easton without anyone on the boat to help him. He'd obviously been successful in finding someone to lead his mules.

Sarah's stomach rumbled again, pulling her thoughts aside. Moving slowly, she left the room and made her way carefully down the winding stairs.

When she entered the kitchen, she found Betsy standing in front of the stove, stirring a kettle of stew. The tantalizing aroma made Sarah's mouth water.

"Did you have a good nap?" Betsy asked, turning to look at Sarah.

Sarah nodded. "I slept longer than I thought I would."

"I'm glad you did. You needed the rest." Betsy motioned to the table, where a gas lantern had been lit. "If you'd like to take a seat, I'll fix you a cup of tea, and we can visit while I finish making supper."

"Don't you want my help?"

"I can manage. Besides, you're supposed to rest."

Sarah pulled out a chair and winced as she sat down. "I can't believe I fell asleep like I did. I haven't slept that hard in ages."

"With the long hours you've been working, you need all the rest you can get." Betsy placed a pot of tea on the table and a cup for Sarah.

"Where are the kids?" Sarah asked as she poured herself some tea.

"Helen and Willis are playing a game in the parlor, but Sammy's not home from school yet."

Sarah frowned. "That's strange. He's always here way before it's time to start supper."

"Maybe he stopped by one of his friend's houses on the way home," Betsy said. "Or maybe the teacher kept him after school."

Sarah's frown deepened. "I hope not. Sammy's always had a mind of his own. I hope he didn't say or do anything to get in trouble with his teacher today." She rose from her seat and glanced out the kitchen window at the darkening sky. It looked like it might rain. "Maybe I should walk over to the schoolhouse and see if he's there. It'll be better than sitting here worrying about him."

"If anyone's going to the schoolhouse, it'll be me," Betsy said with a shake of her head. "The stew's simmering and should be okay, and when I get back, I'll fix some of that dough dab bread you often make to go with it. In the meantime, why don't you go into the parlor and watch the children play?"

"Are you sure you don't mind going after Sammy? If it rains you could get awfully wet."

Betsy smiled. "It wouldn't be the first time I got caught in a downpour, and a little water won't hurt me."

"Oh, all right," Sarah finally agreed. She just hoped Sammy wasn't in trouble with his teacher.

A few drops of water splattered Elias's arm, and he realized that it had started to rain. "Oh great, this is not what I need." He glanced at the towpath to see how Sammy was doing. The poor little fellow was limping and must have developed a blister from walking all day. Either that or he'd managed to get a rock in his boot. The boy had never complained even once, and had kept moving at a pretty good pace. The little bit Sammy had been taught about leading mules had obviously stuck, for Dolly and Daisy behaved as well for Sammy as they had for Bobby.

I still can't believe Sammy's mother agreed to let him go with me, Elias thought. *She'd seemed so dead set against it at first. Guess after she thought things through, she decided that Sammy was up to the task.*

Elias's stomach growled noisily. *I'd better fix us something to eat,* he decided. *If it keeps raining like this, I may as well stop for the night.*

"Hold up the mules!" Elias called to Sammy. "You can tie them to that tree over there, and then be ready to tie off the boat when I throw you the rope."

Sammy did as he was told, and then Elias steered the boat close to shore and set the wooden plank in place.

"What are we stoppin' for?" Sammy asked. "Did I do somethin' wrong?"

"No, not at all. You've done real well today. We need to eat supper, and since it's raining, I thought this would be a good time to stop." He pointed to Sammy's right foot. "I noticed you were limping. Do you have a blister on your foot?"

Sammy nodded. "I think so. Maybe tomorrow I'll walk in my bare feet."

Elias shook his head. "That's not a good idea. You might come across some poisonous snake on the path. Come aboard now. I've got some ointment on the boat for cuts, so I'll put some of that on your blister and then wrap it real good."

"That's nice of you, Mr. Brooks. You're a good man, just like my papa was."

Elias smiled. "You know, I'd like it if you'd leave out the 'Mr. Brooks' part, and just call me Elias."

Sammy grinned up at him. "You're a nice man, Elias."

As Betsy left the schoolhouse, a feeling of concern welled in her chest. Mabel Clark, the teacher, had been cleaning the blackboards when Betsy arrived, and when asked about Sammy, she'd explained that the boy hadn't been at school.

So, if he didn't go to school, where did he go when he left Sarah's house this morning? Betsy asked herself. *Did he decide to go fishing in the canal, or could he have gone into the woods to play? I need to go home and talk to William about this,* she decided. *Sure don't want to go back and tell Sarah her son is missing. At least not until we've looked for him.*

Betsy hurried her steps, and when she entered the parsonage, she was relieved to find William sitting at his desk, studying his sermon for Sunday.

"Sammy Turner's missing," she said, touching William's shoulder. "I need your help finding him."

William's forehead creased. "Did you look at the schoolhouse?"

"I did, but Mabel said Sammy never came to school, and I know for a fact that he hasn't been home all day."

William pushed his chair aside and stood. "That's not good. You're right; we need to look for him."

For the next hour, Betsy and William went up and down the streets of Walnutport, searching for Sammy and asking everyone they met if they'd seen any sign of the boy. No one had, and Betsy's concerns turned to fear. "What if he went fishing and fell in the canal?" she asked William. "What if he—"

William held up his hand. "Let's not think the worst. We need to keep looking."

"Where else shall we look?"

"I think we should check at Cooper's store. Sammy might have gone there to play with his cousins."

"Do you think he'd do that without asking his mother?"

William shrugged. "I'm not a father yet, so I'm no expert on children, but I wouldn't be surprised by anything Sammy might do. He's always been a challenge for Sarah, and his curiosity has sometimes gotten him in trouble."

"That's true, but if he'd gone to the store to play with his cousins, wouldn't Kelly or Mike have let Sarah know?"

William turned his hands palms up. "Not if they

thought he'd gotten his mother's permission to come over."

"But surely they know Sarah would never allow Sammy to skip school so he could play."

"Maybe he found something else to do during school hours and then went over to the Coopers' later in the day."

"Well, it's worth checking anyway," Betsy said. "Should we walk or go back home and get our horse and buckboard?"

"We may as well walk, because we're at the end of town now, and it would take too much time to get the horse hitched to the buckboard."

"You've got a point." Betsy clasped William's arm, and they hurried toward the store, which had been built close to the canal, and was only a short distance from the lock tender's house.

When it came into view, Betsy noticed several children playing in the side yard near the Coopers' house, which was connected to the back of their store. She didn't, however, see Sammy among the children there.

"Should we check at the house or the store?" she asked William.

"Let's start with the store, because I'm sure it's still open."

When they entered the store, they found Mike behind the counter, waiting on Patrick O'Grady, the town's able-bodied blacksmith. Patrick, who was in his early thirties and still single, had wavy red hair and pale blue eyes—obvious traits from his Irish heritage. When they stepped up to the counter, he turned and gave them a nod. "I talked to Gus Stevens at the livery stable, and he said you gave a fine sermon last Sunday, Preacher," Patrick said with a smile. "Gus said it got him to thinkin' that he oughta spend less time worryin' and more time prayin'."

"I'm glad Gus took something away from the sermon," William said. "I deliberated for a while on what I should preach last Sunday, but that was the sermon the Lord laid on my heart." His brows furrowed above his finely chiseled nose. "We'd like to have you join us in church sometime, Patrick."

"Maybe someday; we'll see," Patrick mumbled.

Betsy cleared her throat and nudged William's arm. "Did you want to ask Mike about Sammy, or should I?"

William's face turned red. "Oh, sorry. I forgot for a minute what we came here for. That happens to me sometimes when I'm talking about the Lord's work."

"What can I help you with?" Mike asked after he'd handed Patrick his purchases.

"Sammy's missing," Betsy said before William could even open his mouth. "His teacher said he didn't go to school today, and William and I have looked all over town for him."

"He's probably sitting along the bank of the

canal someplace with his fishin' pole," Patrick called over his shoulder as he headed out the door. "That's what I used to do when I was his age." The door clicked shut behind Patrick.

"Sammy's not missing," Mike said. "I know exactly where he is."

A sense of relief flooded Betsy's soul. "Where?"

"He's walking the towpath, leading Elias's mules."

William's jaw dropped, and Betsy sucked in her breath. "Are—are you sure about that?"

Mike gave a nod. "Elias and Sammy were in the store earlier, and Sammy told Elias that his mother gave her permission for him to lead the mules."

Betsy clutched William's arm. "Sarah did not give Sammy permission to go with Elias. She told him in no uncertain terms that he couldn't go."

"I can't believe Sammy would lie to Elias like that," William said.

"We've got to go after him." Betsy's voice raised a notch. "We've got to bring him back to Sarah!"

"When they left here it was still early," Mike said. "They could be halfway to Easton by now. Elias seems like a very nice man. I'm sure Sammy will be fine with him."

Betsy glared at Mike. "Are you suggesting that we just let the boy walk to and from Easton, leading two mules who could easily trample him to death?"

"I'm well-acquainted with Elias's mules. He put them up in my stable when he docked his boat here for the night a week or so ago." Mike shook his head. "They were two of the most docile mules I've ever met, so I'm sure they won't harm Sammy in any way."

"Humph!" Betsy folded her arms. "Mules can kick and bite, even the very tame ones. Why I remember once when I was girl, one of the young mule drivers ended up with a broken leg because a mule kicked him."

"I think we need to go over to Sarah's and tell her where Sammy is," William said. "After that, we'll decide what we should do about the situation."

Betsy nodded and drew in a deep breath. She dreaded telling Sarah what had happened to Sammy.

Chapter 11

Since the rain hadn't let up, Elias decided to stay put for the night, because he didn't want Sammy to get soaked. Even though most of the canal boats ran as many as eighteen hours a day, Elias felt that walking the mules that many hours was out of the question for such a young boy. Sammy looked so tired, Elias was afraid the boy might drop. And with a sore foot, asking him to walk any farther tonight would be just plain stupid.

"Let's go down below," Elias told the boy. "I'll cut a loaf of bread and heat us some bean soup."

Sammy nodded eagerly. "I am kinda hungry. Fact is, I think I could eat the whole loaf of bread."

Elias smiled and led the way to the galley, furnished with the barest of essentials. A small kitchen table was covered with oilcloth, and four stools were stored under the table when not in use. A black, coal-burning stove sat off to one side, and a kerosene lamp had been placed in a bracket on the wall over the table.

Elias set a pan of water on the stove to boil and then added some soaked navy beans, diced carrots, a cut-up onion, a hunk of salt pork, and just enough salt and pepper to season the soup. While it cooked, he cut some bread. Then after a short prayer, he and Sammy each had a piece.

"Have you ever been on a canal boat before?" Elias asked the boy.

Sammy nodded. "I was on my Grandpa McGregor's boat a few times, but of course, Mama wouldn't let me ride very far with him. Said she didn't want me gettin' used to the idea of canalin'."

"Why's that?"

"Mama's always said that she hates the canal. Says it took my papa, and that it's given her nothin' but misery."

"Does your grandpa still have his boat?" Elias asked, feeling the need for a change of subject.

Sammy shook his head. "He sold it and moved to Easton after Grandma died."

"That's too bad."

Sammy leaned his elbows on the table and stared at Elias. "Can I ask ya a question?"

"Sure."

"I've been wonderin' about that red mark on your face. Did ya burn yourself or somethin'?"

Elias shook his head. "I was born with it."

"Does it hurt?"

"No, not at all."

"Can I touch it?"

In all Elias's twenty-eight years, he'd had lots of people ask about the birthmark, stare at him curiously, and even make fun of him, but he'd never had anyone ask if he could touch it. "I . . . uh . . . guess it'd be okay," he said.

Sammy leaned over and placed his hand on Elias's cheek. "It feels like skin—same as any other."

A smile tugged at the corners of Elias's mouth. "Yes, Sammy, it's just a different color from the rest of my skin."

Sammy nodded and leaned back in his chair, lacing his fingers behind his head. "Can I ask ya another question?"

"Sure."

"My other grandma used to live with us, but she's goin' blind and had to move to Easton awhile back. I was wonderin' if we could stop and see her there."

Elias shook his head. "I'm sorry, Sammy, but I don't know where your grandma lives. Even if I did, I couldn't leave my boat and mules unattended to take you there." He gave Sammy's shoulder a squeeze. "Maybe you'll get to Easton to see her some other time."

Sammy stared down at his plate and mumbled, "I sure hope so."

Elias pushed the loaf of bread toward Sammy. "Would you like another piece?"

"Think I'd better wait for the soup. Wouldn't wanna eat up all your bread."

"That's okay. There's plenty." Elias cut Sammy another piece of bread; then he went to the small cabin where he slept and got out his accordion.

"Ever heard one of these?" he asked the boy.

"Nope, but the preacher's wife plays the zither and the organ."

"Well, this is called an accordion. It has keys and bellows, sort of like an organ." Elias slipped the straps over his shoulders. "Now here's a song just for you, Sammy. It's called 'Go Along Mule.' "

Elias began to play and sing: *I've got a mule, she's such a fool; she never pays me no heed. I'll build a fire beneath her tail, and then she'll show me some speed.*

Sammy laughed and joined Elias as they sang the song together.

What a joy it was for Elias to spend time with

this easygoing young lad. It made him long to be a father.

But that's just an impossible dream, Elias thought as he touched the red mark on his face. *Surely no decent woman would want someone as ugly as me.*

"Mama, I'm hungry." Willis, who sat at the table beside Sarah as she drank a cup of tea, tugged on her sleeve. "Is it time for supper yet?"

Sarah glanced at the windup clock sitting on the counter across the room. It was time for supper, but she didn't want to eat until Sammy got home. She couldn't figure out why he wasn't here yet. Even if he'd been kept after school, he should have been home by now.

Willis gave Sarah's sleeve another tug. "Mama, I'm hungry."

"We'll eat supper as soon as Betsy gets back here with Sammy." Sarah rose from her chair. "Would you like a piece of jelly bread to tide you over?"

Willis bobbed his head and then pointed to his little sister, who was sitting on the floor, petting Bristle Face. "I think Helen would like one, too."

Sarah winced when she picked up a knife to butter the bread. Even a simple movement caused her ribs to ache.

She'd just given the children some bread spread with jelly and a glass of milk when the back door swung open and Ned stepped in. "If supper's ready, I can eat real quick and get back outside, 'cause the last canaler who went through said there were three more boats comin' up the canal behind him."

"Let me check on the stew." Sarah lifted the lid on the kettle and poked a potato with a fork. "It seems to be done enough, so as soon you wash up I'll dish you and the kids a bowl and then you can eat."

"I already washed in the canal."

"Oh, I see. Well, have a seat then, and I'll get you some stew."

"What about you? Ain't you gonna eat with us?"

She shook her head. "I'll wait until Sammy gets home."

"Didn't realize he wasn't here." Ned pulled his fingers down the length of his bristly face. "Where'd the boy go?"

She shrugged. "I don't know. I think he may have been kept after school."

Ned grunted as he took a seat at the table. "Can't tell ya how many times I was kept after school when I was a boy. 'Course, I only had a few years of learnin' before I started workin' for my pappy." He reached for a piece of bread and slathered it with some of the strawberry jelly Maria had made before her eyesight had gotten so bad. "I was eight years old when I started leadin' the mules that pulled Pappy's boat."

Sarah cringed. She wouldn't even think of taking Sammy out of school so he could walk the rutted towpath for hours on end, the way she and Kelly had done when they were girls. "Didn't you go to school at all after you began walking the mules?" she questioned.

"Went durin' the colder months when the canal was shut down, but by the time I was twelve, I'd begun cuttin' ice with Pappy during the winter. Then in the spring when the boats started up again, I'd quit school and start walkin' the mules." Ned puffed out his chest. "Got pretty good at it, too, I might add."

Sarah was glad she and Kelly had been allowed to attend school during the winter months. Mama had taught them some on the boat before bedtime, too, so at least they'd gotten a fairly good education.

Turning her thoughts aside, Sarah ladled some stew into three bowls and set them on the table. She was about to tell the children to bow their heads for prayer when the back door opened. Betsy and Pastor William stepped in. The solemn look on Betsy's face sent a chill up Sarah's spine.

"What's wrong?" she asked fearfully. "Didn't you find Sammy?"

Pastor William shook his head. "No, but we know where he is."

"Wh–where is he?"

"He's with Elias—leading his mules."

75

Sarah gasped and grabbed the back of a chair for support. "But how can that be? This morning I specifically told him that he couldn't lead those mules, and Elias heard me say it, too." She looked at Pastor William. "When Elias's boat disappeared, I thought you must have found a mule driver for him in town."

He shook his head. "I couldn't find anyone, and when I went to the place where Elias had tied up his boat, he was gone. So I figured he must have found someone on his own."

White-hot anger boiled inside Sarah, and she clenched her fists in frustration, until her nails dug into her palms. "How could that man have taken my son when he knew I didn't want Sammy to go?"

Betsy shook her head. "That's not how it happened, Sarah. William and I just spoke to Mike, and he heard what Sammy said to Elias at the store this morning."

Sarah's eyebrows squeezed together. "What are you talking about? I sent Sammy to school, and Elias was going to wait until Pastor William found someone to lead his mules. How could Mike have heard Sammy talking to Elias at the store?"

Betsy explained about the conversation that had taken place between Elias and Sammy. "Apparently, Sammy never went to school. Instead, he convinced Elias that you'd changed

76

your mind and had given your permission for Sammy to go with him."

Sarah stomped her foot, and winced when a jolt of pain shot through her ribs. "I never changed my mind, and I can't imagine that Sammy would lie and say that I had."

"So what are you sayin'?" Ned spoke up. "Are you sayin' that the storekeeper was lyin'?"

"I'm not saying that at all. What I think is that Elias was so desperate for someone to lead his mules that he talked Sammy into going with him. Who knows, maybe he even told Sammy that he'd spoken with me again, and that I'd said it was all right for him to go."

Ned shook his head. "Elias would never do nothin' like that. He's a good man—and an honest one, to boot."

Sarah clasped Pastor William's arm. "Would you go after my boy and bring him home?"

Pastor William slowly shook his head. "They left hours ago, Sarah. They're probably halfway to Easton by now. I think the best thing we can do is trust God to take care of Sammy and wait for him to come home."

Sarah blinked back tears that were stinging her eyes and sank into a chair at the table with a moan.

"Not to worry," Ned said. "Elias will take good care of your boy."

Sarah couldn't even speak around the lump in her throat. She was worried sick and didn't know

Elias well enough to have any confidence that he'd take proper care of her boy. Besides, there were so many things that could happen while he was leading the mules. He could get kicked or bitten by one of those stubborn beasts. He could collapse from the exhaustion of walking too many hours. She remembered how when she was a girl working for her father, she'd once seen a young boy get dragged by his mule right over one of the lockgates. It was a frightening thing to watch, and it was a miracle the boy hadn't drowned in the canal.

"I think what we all need to do is hold hands and offer a prayer for Elias and Sammy," Pastor William suggested.

"You can count me out of the prayer," Ned said. "I ain't into all that religious stuff!"

Pastor William gave Ned's shoulder a squeeze. "The Lord never makes a man do anything against his will, so if you're not comfortable with praying you can just sit and listen. How's that sound?"

Ned gave a nod. "Suits me just fine."

Pastor William joined hands with Sarah and Betsy. "Heavenly Father," he prayed, "please be with Elias and Sammy wherever they are right now. Give them a safe trip to Easton and back, and let them know that You are right there with them. Be with Sarah and her children here, and give her a sense of peace, knowing that You'll watch over her son and bring him safely back home. Amen."

Sarah sniffed as tears rolled down her hot cheeks, wishing once again that there might be some way to get her children away from the canal.

Chapter 12

After spending a night on the canal near Kimmet's Lock, about fourteen miles from Walnutport, Elias was able to make his coal delivery to Easton by late afternoon the following day. They'd headed out as soon as the boat was unloaded and had gone as far as the Catasauqua Lock and then spent that night. They'd gotten an early start this morning, and if all went well, they should be back at Walnutport before noon.

It had rained off and on yesterday, and even though the sun was out now, the towpath was quite muddy. Elias hoped it wouldn't slow them down too much. He alternated between looking up ahead as he steered the boat and keeping an eye on Sammy as he led the mules.

He frowned when he realized that Sammy's trousers were caked with mud. He wished he could wash the boy's clothes before he dropped him off at home, but if he took time for that, they'd be even later getting back to Walnutport. Besides, the sun wasn't warm enough to dry the clothes.

As they continued to travel, Elias reflected on

the time he'd spent with Sammy and realized he was going to miss the boy when he returned him to his family. Last night, they'd visited during supper again, and afterward, Elias had played the accordion while they sang. Just before they'd gone to bed, Elias had told Sammy that when they got back to Walnutport, he would pay him for walking the mules. Sammy had smiled and said he planned to use the money to buy his mother a birthday present, because this coming Sunday was her birthday.

That boy is sure thoughtful, Elias thought. *Most kids Sammy's age only think of themselves. He must love his mother very much.*

"Get up there! Haw! Haw!"

Elias jerked his head to the left and grimaced when he saw Sammy slipping and sliding along the muddy towpath, as he struggled to keep the mules moving. They balked whenever they came to a puddle, and Sammy had to lead them around it, no matter how small the puddle of water was. At the rate they were going, it would be late in the day before they made it back to Walnutport.

Elias cupped his hands around his mouth. "Are you doing okay, Sammy? Do you need to stop for a while?"

"I'm fine. Just need to show these stubborn mules who's boss." Sammy tipped his head back and began to sing, *"I've got a mule, she's such a fool, she never pays me no heed. I'll build a fire under her tail, and then she'll show me some speed."*

Elias chuckled. The boy had determination, as well as a sense of humor—exactly what was needed here on the canal.

When Betsy showed up at Sarah's much later than usual that morning, Sarah noticed right away that she looked pale and seemed kind of shaky.

"What's wrong?" Sarah asked. "Has something happened?"

Betsy shook her head. "I'm just feeling a bit queasy this morning. I think I might be coming down with the flu. If that's the case, then I probably shouldn't be here today. I wouldn't want to expose you and the children, but at the same time I don't want to leave you alone all day when I know you're still hurting."

"I'm feeling better now, so if you're not well, then you need to go home and rest."

Betsy hesitated a minute. "I . . . I don't suppose Sammy's come home yet."

Sarah slowly shook her head. "I'm trying not to worry, but it isn't easy."

"I'm sure it's not, but you need to keep trusting the Lord." Betsy offered Sarah a smile. "When Sammy does get home, send him over to the parsonage to let me know. That way I can spread the word to those who've been praying for him."

"I will, and if you're not feeling up to watching

my kids when I start working again, let me know, and I'll see if Kelly's available for a few hours to help out."

"I'm sure I'll be fine in a day or so." Betsy placed both hands against her stomach. "It could even be something I ate last night that didn't agree with me." She turned and started down the stairs, calling over her shoulder, "See you soon, Sarah."

When Sarah returned to the kitchen she discovered that Willis and Helen had gotten out some of her pots and pans and had them strewn all over the kitchen floor.

"Pick those up and put them away!" Sarah shouted.

Willis blinked his eyes rapidly, and Helen started to howl.

Sarah's head began to pound. Everything seemed to bother her more since Sammy had taken off with Elias. If she only knew whether he was safe or not. If he'd just come home to her now.

"I'll tell you what," she said to the children in a much softer tone. "If you two will put the pots and pans away I'll take you for a walk to Aunt Kelly and Uncle Mike's store."

"Can we have a peppermint stick?" Willis wanted to know.

Sarah nodded. "If you do as I say and pick up the pots and pans."

Willis went to work immediately, and even

Helen put a few of the pans back in the cupboard. When they were done, Sarah got their jackets and led them out the door.

As they walked the towpath, Sarah felt a cool morning breeze blowing through the canal that ran north and south.

She glanced at the hills surrounding Walnutport and noticed how green they were. Spring was definitely here, and it wouldn't be long before the flowers she'd planted near the house would be in full bloom.

"Look, Mama . . . a quack, quack." Helen pointed to a pair of mallard ducks floating gracefully on the canal.

"And look over there," Willis said, pointing to a bushy-tailed squirrel running through the grassy area on one side of the towpath.

Before Sarah could respond, Willis darted through the grass, giving the poor squirrel a merry chase. Helen tried to join him, but Sarah took hold of her hand.

"Leave that squirrel alone, Willis," Sarah scolded. "If we don't keep walking, we'll never get to the store."

Willis halted the chase and joined Sarah and Helen on the path again.

When they entered the store, the children went immediately to the candy counter, which was their favorite place.

"What can I do for the two of you?" Mike asked

as he stepped out from behind the counter where he waited on customers.

"Candy! Candy!" Helen shouted. She hopped up and down on her toes, while Willis pressed his nose against the glass and peered at the candy.

Mike looked at Sarah and chuckled. "These two seem pretty eager today. Did you say they could have some candy?"

"Yes, I did," Sarah replied. "I said they could have a peppermint stick."

"Alright, then." Mike opened the back of the candy counter and pulled out the glass jar full of peppermint sticks. Then he came around, knelt beside the children, and handed them each one. "Anna and Marcus are in the house," he said. "Why don't the two of you go over there and play awhile?"

The children didn't have to be asked twice. They each took a lick from their peppermint sticks and scurried through the door leading to Mike and Kelly's house.

Sarah pulled some money from her apron pocket and handed it to Mike.

"What's that for?" he asked.

"The kids' peppermint sticks."

He shook his head. "No way; the candy's my treat."

She smiled. "Thank you." Her kids were fortunate to have such a nice uncle, and Sarah was glad that Kelly had found such a considerate husband.

"How are your ribs feeling?" Mike asked.

"They don't hurt quite so much, but I'd feel a lot better if Sammy would come home."

"I'm sure he'll be here soon. Elias has probably been taking his time so he doesn't wear Sammy out."

"Humph! Sammy's too young and inexperienced to be leading a pair of unpredictable mules. He shouldn't have gone with Elias at all!"

"You're right, but I'm sure he'll be fine."

"Is Kelly in the house or her studio?" Sarah asked, changing the subject. If she kept talking about Sammy she'd get all worked up.

"She's in her studio, painting. Why don't you visit with her awhile? I'm sure she'd be glad to see you."

"Okay." Sarah started in the direction of the adjoining art studio, when she heard the familiar moaning of a conch shell. She moved quickly to the front window. "Maybe that's Elias and Sammy." She stepped outside and waited until the boat came around the bend, but when it came into her line of vision, she realized it was traveling toward Easton, so it couldn't be them.

She was just about to step back into the store, when Patrick O'Grady, the town's blacksmith, showed up.

"Top of the mornin', Sarah," he said, tipping the straw hat he wore over his curly red hair. "How are you doin' this fine spring day?"

"I've been better," she mumbled.

"I heard about the fall you took a few days ago and have been wonderin' how you were doin'. Fact is, I'd planned to come by your place yesterday, but I got so busy in my shop that I couldn't get away."

"I'm doing some better, and my ribs aren't quite so sore."

"That's good to hear." He grinned, and the deep dimples in his cheeks seemed to be winking at her. "Say, I was wondering. Would you and your youngsters be interested in goin' on a picnic with me this Sunday? Thought maybe we could start out in the morning and do some fishin' in the canal before we eat."

Sarah's fingers tightened around the edge of her jacket. "Well, uh . . . we always go to church on Sundays."

"Oh yeah, that's right. Well, how about we get together later in the day?"

"Maybe some other time—when my ribs are feeling better, and my boy Sammy's back home."

"Where'd he go?"

Sarah explained about Sammy's unexpected trip with Elias and ended it by saying, "So I don't feel that I can go anywhere until my boy's home safe and sound."

"When I was in here the other day I heard the preacher and his wife say they'd been lookin' for Sammy. But I figured the boy had probably just gone off fishin' somewhere." Patrick's nose wrinkled as he gave an undignified snort. "What in the world was that boatman thinking? He had no right to take off with a kid as young as Sammy."

"I've been thinking the very same thing."

Another conch shell blew, and a few minutes later a boat came into view. Sarah's heart gave a lurch. It was Elias's boat, and there was Sammy, leading the mules.

As the boat pulled up to a wooden post near the store, Sarah lifted the edge of her skirt and raced through the tall grass, ready to give both Elias and Sammy a piece of her mind.

Chapter 13

"*O*h, I'm so glad you're back." Sarah pulled Sammy close and hugged him tightly. "I was worried sick about you."

When Sammy looked up at her, his eyes shone brightly. "I did real good leadin' the mules; Elias said so." He patted the pocket in his trousers. "He paid me for helpin' him, too."

Sarah looked up at Elias and shook her finger, the way she often did when one of her children had done something wrong. "What were you thinking, taking off with my boy like that—and without even getting my permission?"

Elias's face turned red, matching the birthmark

on his cheek. "But I . . . I thought—that is, I mean, Sammy said you'd given him your permission."

Sarah shook her head. "I told him no. You were right there when I said it, too."

"I realize that, but Sammy said you'd changed your mind, and . . ."

Sarah turned back to Sammy. "Did you lie to Elias and tell him I said it was okay for you to lead his mules?"

Sammy nodded slowly and dropped his gaze to the ground. "I wanted to earn some money so I could—"

"There's no excuse for lying; I've taught you better than that." Sarah's hands shook as she held them firmly at her sides. "You disobeyed me, and then lied to Elias, and now you'll need to be punished." She pointed to the store. "Go inside and wait for me. I'll be in soon, and then we'll be heading for home."

Sammy's eyes filled with tears. "I'm sorry, Mama. Sure didn't mean to upset ya, but I—"

"Just go into the store; we'll talk about this later. Oh, and please tell Uncle Mike to ask one of his customers from town to let Pastor William and Betsy know that you've come home."

"I can let them know," Elias spoke up. "I have to go into town to check on Bobby, my mule driver, so it'll be right on my way."

"Okay, thanks," Sarah mumbled.

Sammy started to walk away but turned back

and looked up at Elias. "Thanks for all the things ya taught me. I had a real good time."

Elias smiled and nodded. "I had a good time with you, too."

Sammy turned and sprinted to the store.

"I'm really sorry about this," Elias said. "If I'd had any idea that Sammy—"

"Sammy's only a boy. You shouldn't have taken his word. You should have checked with me first."

He nodded. "You're right. In fact, I take the full blame, so please don't be too hard on Sammy."

Irritation welled in Sarah's soul. "Don't tell me how to raise my son. Sammy lied, and he needs a reminder not to do it again."

"You're right, of course. I only meant that it wasn't solely his fault, and I hope you'll take that into consideration."

"I'll consider all that needs to be considered. Now, if you'll excuse me, I need to get my kids and go home." She started to move away, but Elias touched her arm, and she whirled around to face him. "What?"

"How are your ribs? Are they better?"

"They're not fully healed, but I'm sure I can manage to do my work again now."

"Why not give yourself another day or so to heal? I'll be staying here until Monday morning, so Ned may as well continue opening the lock for the rest of the day, and since Sunday's a day of rest it'll give us all a chance to renew."

Sarah considered Elias's suggestion. He really did seem to care about her predicament. "That's fine," she said with a nod. "If I don't have to worry about the lock for the rest of the day it'll give me some time to care for my kids. From the looks of Sammy's trousers and shirt, I'd say he and his clothes both need a good washing."

"We had some rain on the way to Easton, which made the towpath quite muddy."

"Oh, I know all about the muddy towpath. I traipsed through more mud than I care to think about when I was a girl leading my papa's mules."

Elias quirked an eyebrow. "I didn't realize you'd ever been a mule driver. I thought maybe you'd grown up in the lock tender's house."

"No, my husband's folks tended the lock before he took it over, and then after he died, it became my job." Sarah frowned. "I hated walking the towpath when I was a girl, so when I turned eighteen, I ran away with Sam, and we got married. We both worked in Phillipsburg, New Jersey, for a time, before returning here to Walnutport." Sarah didn't know why she was telling Elias all this. She barely knew the man, and it was really none of his business, and yet he seemed so easy to talk to and seemed to be interested in what she was saying. "I'd better go," she murmured. "Thanks for bringing Sammy home safe." Sarah turned and hurried toward the store.

• • •

Elias, still feeling bad about taking Sammy without checking with Sarah first, headed over to the lock to see Ned. He found him sitting on a rock close to the canal, with a fishing pole in his hand.

"I saw your boat pull in," Ned said when Elias took a seat on the ground next to him. "Sure took ya long enough to get up to Easton and back here again."

"Since Sammy's not an experienced mule driver, I didn't want to push him too hard. We also had some rainy weather to deal with."

Ned grunted. "I heard you'd taken the kid along. His mama wasn't too happy about that, ya know. In fact, I had to hear about it several times."

"Yes, I'm sure. I've apologized to Sarah for taking Sammy's word and not checking with her first." Elias frowned. "I still don't understand why he lied to me."

Ned spit a wad of chewing tobacco into the canal. "Lyin's what kids do best." He snorted. "'Course I'm sure someone as good as you has never told a lie in his life."

"I'm not perfect, and I think everyone's lied at some time or another. The Bible says in Romans 3:23, 'For all have sinned, and come short of the glory of God.' "

Ned spat again. "Don't start preachin' to me, now. I ain't in the mood."

"I wasn't preaching. I was just saying that everyone has sinned, which means that most people have told a lie or two."

"Yeah, whatever."

Elias decided it was time for a change in conversation. "I see you're making good use of your time when you're not bringing a boat through the lock," he said, motioning to the fishing pole in Ned's hand.

"Yep. Thought I might catch me a mess of fish for supper tonight. 'Course I'd figured on offerin' them to Sarah, since she's been feedin' me while you've been gone. Now that you're back, and since Sarah's feelin' better, I'd better quit fishin' so we can be on our way to Mauch Chunk."

Elias shook his head. "I've decided to stay here for the rest of today and Sunday, of course. We'll head out on Monday morning."

Ned's bushy eyebrows lifted high on his forehead. "And waste the rest of a perfectly good day? Are ya crazy, man?"

"No, I'm not crazy, and need I remind you that you're working for me, not the other way around? So I'd appreciate it if you just accepted my decision without grumbling about it."

"But why would ya wanna hang around here all day when you've got a load of coal to pick up?"

"So you can continue opening the lock. I think

Sarah needs an extra day or so to allow her ribs to heal sufficiently. If we stay here until Monday, it'll give me a chance to visit the church in Walnutport, too."

Ned squinted his beady eyes, and his thin lips compressed. "Guess if you wanna go to church, that's your decision, but don't look for me to tag along."

Elias shrugged. "That's entirely up to you." He pulled himself to his feet. "We'll eat on the boat tonight, so if you catch any fish, we can have them for supper."

"Mike Cooper loaned me this fishin' pole, since mine was on your boat. Why don't ya go over to his store and see if he's got another pole you can use? That way we'll have twice as many fish for supper."

"It's tempting, but I need to go over to the boardinghouse where we left Bobby with his aunt Martha and see if he's feeling better and will be ready to lead the mules on Monday morning. You haven't heard anything about how the boy's doing, have you?"

Ned shook his head. "Been too busy here to check on him."

"Okay. After I inquire about Bobby, I need to stop by the preacher's house and let him and his wife know that Sammy made it home okay. I'll either see you back here or at the boat."

"Sure thing, boss. Whatever you say."

Elias shook his head as he walked away. He hoped that someday Ned might be won to the Lord, but he wouldn't push. He'd just allow things to come naturally and let the Lord lead.

Chapter 14

On Sunday morning as Sarah sat on one of the wooden pews in church with her children, she was surprised to see Elias enter the sanctuary and take a seat in the pew across from her. As the first song, "We Have an Anchor," was announced, everyone stood. Sammy slipped quickly past Sarah and darted across the aisle to stand beside Elias.

Sarah gritted her teeth. She wasn't one bit happy about this but didn't make a move to bring him back to her pew because she figured he might balk. She sure didn't want to create a scene during church.

Sammy was a spirited child with a mind of his own. He obviously preferred to sit with Elias instead of her.

Maybe he's still angry about the paddling I gave him for lying yesterday, Sarah thought. *I don't think he realized that it hurt me more than it did him. But he needed to learn that lying is not acceptable.*

From past experience, Sarah knew that a strong lecture or even some extra chores, wouldn't have been enough to get Sammy's attention and help him remember not to tell more lies.

Sarah focused her thoughts back to the song. The words were fitting for this group of people who lived along the canal. She needed the reminder that even when the storms of life threatened to overtake her, Jesus was the anchor she could count on.

When the song ended, everyone sat down. Then Pastor William moved over to stand beside Betsy at the organ. They sang a duet, "Tell It to Jesus."

Sarah leaned against the back of her pew and closed her eyes as she took the words of the song to heart.

"Are you weary, are you heavy-hearted? Tell it to Jesus; tell it to Jesus. Are you grieving over joys departed? Tell it to Jesus alone."

Sarah was indeed, weary. She'd been weary ever since Sam's passing. Even on Sundays, her only day of rest, she was sometimes so tired she could hardly keep her eyes open. She was also grieving over joys departed because it seemed like she and Sam had only had a few short years of real happiness in their marriage.

When she'd first run away and married him, it had been to get away from the canal and her father's harsh ways. Then, after they'd moved to New Jersey and taken jobs, Sam had started drinking and had lost his job. Eventually, he'd walked out on Sarah and little Sammy. It wasn't until Sarah moved back to the canal to live with her folks that Sam had finally come to his senses and begged her to give him a second chance.

They'd moved into his folks' house, and Sam had tended the lock with his dad while Sarah helped Sam's mother bake bread to sell to the boatmen. After Sam's father died, Maria moved to Easton to live with Roger. Sam took over the lock tender's responsibilities, and Sarah started doing laundry for the boatmen to help with their finances.

Soon after that, Sam began attending church and had made a sincere commitment to the Lord. From that point on, they'd had the kind of marriage God intended for a husband and wife. During the short time before Sam's death, he'd been a loving husband and father. If only he hadn't been snatched away. If things could have stayed the way they were. Then Sarah wouldn't be faced with the responsibility of raising three children on her own, while trying to make a living doing something she'd rather not do.

"Now if you'll turn in your Bibles to First Peter, we'll be reading from chapter five, verse seven," Pastor William announced.

Sarah's eyes snapped open. She'd been so consumed with her thoughts that she hadn't even realized Betsy and Pastor William had finished their song.

She opened her Bible and found the scripture

passage in 1 Peter. As Pastor William read the verse, she followed along: *"Casting all your care upon him; for he careth for you."*

Sarah needed that reminder. She knew she should read a few verses of scripture every day if she was going to make it through the storms of life. The Bible was full of wisdom, and she was reminded of Psalm 119:105 that said God's Word was a lamp unto her feet and a light unto her path.

Elias glanced at Sammy, sitting so close to him that their arms touched, and he smiled. During the short time he and the boy had spent together on the trip to and from Easton, they'd established a bond. Elias didn't know if it was because Sammy missed his father and needed a man in his life, or if it was because he, wishing to be a father, had bonded with the boy. In any case, it appeared Sammy liked being with Elias, or he wouldn't have left his seat and come over here to sit beside him.

I wonder how his mother feels about that. Elias glanced across the aisle at Sarah, who seemed to be listening intently to the pastor's message. He wondered if Sammy had been able to buy his mother a birthday present, like he'd wanted to do. He also wondered if Sammy had been punished for lying. No doubt he had, since Sarah had been so upset about it. Even though Elias didn't know Sarah very well, she seemed like a good mother who loved her children and wanted the best for them. Sometimes that included discipline—or as Elias's mother used to say when he was a boy: *"I'm punishing you for your own good, and someday you'll thank me for it."*

Elias wasn't sure he'd ever felt thankful for the spankings he'd gotten, but he knew that reasonable discipline was necessary in order to teach children right from wrong.

He glanced around the room at the group who'd come to worship the Lord this fine spring morning. Being in church with these simple folk who didn't put on airs like some of the people in his church back home gave him a sense of belonging. He saw sincerity on their faces, not pride or holier-than-thou expressions. Maybe it was because the people who attended the Walnutport Community Church were hardworking, plain folks, who didn't put on airs or judge a man by how much money he made or how powerful he'd become. *"A man's life is judged not on the things he has but on the things he does,"* Elias's grandfather used to say.

Elias turned his attention to the Bible in his hands, and the words on the page blurred as tears clouded his vision. Grandpa had been a good man with a heart for people, and Elias missed him.

If only Father could be as caring and understanding as Grandpa used to be, Elias thought ruefully. He'd never understood how the son of such an endearing man could turn out so cold and unfeeling. If not for the religious upbringing Elias's mother had given him, along with the godly influence of his grandfather, Elias might never have found a personal relationship with the Lord.

"And now, let us stand for our closing hymn, 'Rescue the Perishing.' "

Elias pushed his thoughts aside, realizing that the pastor's sermon had ended, and their young song leader now stood behind the pulpit, while the pastor made his way to the back of the room to greet everyone at the close of the service.

When the song ended, Sammy looked up at Elias and said, "I'm glad you're here today. I didn't think I'd get to see ya before ya headed up the canal to Mauch Chunk."

Elias smiled. "I decided to hang around Walnutport so I could visit the church here."

Sammy grinned. "Sure glad ya did."

"Is everything all right between you and your mother?" Elias asked.

Sammy bobbed his head. " 'Course she paddled my backside for tellin' ya she said it was okay for me to lead your mules." He clasped Elias's hand. "It was worth the paddlin' to be able to spend those two days with ya, though."

Elias ruffled the boy's thick blond hair. "I'm glad we could be together, but it wasn't right to lie."

"I know, and I won't do it again."

"That's good to hear."

"Can we talk about somethin' else now?"

"Of course."

"Know what I think?"

"What's that?"

"I think you oughta bring your accordion to church sometime."

Elias smiled. "Maybe I'll talk to the pastor about that."

Sarah and her two youngest children stepped up to Elias, and she touched Sammy's shoulder. "Would you please take Willis and Helen outside and wait for me? I'd like to speak to Elias for a minute."

Sammy hesitated, but when Elias gave his shoulder a squeeze, the boy finally nodded.

Sarah waited until the children had left the church; then she moved closer to Elias. "I'm sorry for my harsh words yesterday. I was very upset when I discovered that Sammy had taken off with you, and I needed someone to blame."

Elias nodded. "I understand, and you were right—I shouldn't have taken Sammy's word. I should have checked with you first."

"There's one more thing I wanted to say," she said, lowering her voice.

"What's that?"

"I'd appreciate it if you didn't encourage my boy to take an interest in working on the canal. I don't want him getting any ideas about becoming a mule driver or even a boatman when he grows up."

Elias's forehead wrinkled. "I'd never try to influence Sammy in any way. And as far as him becoming a boatman, with the way things are going, by the time he grows up, the canal boats might not even be running."

"You're probably right, and I really appreciate your understanding."

Sarah moved away, and she stopped at the back of the church to talk to Pastor William and his wife.

Elias's heart clenched, realizing how difficult it must be for her raising three children alone and not wanting her oldest boy to look to the canal for work.

As Elias moved toward the back of the church, he was greeted by the storekeeper's wife, Kelly, whom he'd only met briefly the first time he'd stopped at their store.

"It's nice to see you in church today," she said with a friendly smile. "We hope you'll join us whenever you're in the area."

"Yes, I plan to do that. I enjoyed the service."

"I spoke to my sister, Sarah, before the service began, and she said she's feeling up to taking care of the lock again. So I assume you'll be heading on up the canal in the morning?"

He gave a nod. "I didn't realize Sarah was your sister."

"Yep. She's my older sister by a few years, and we're very close.

"And speaking of her," Kelly continued, "Betsy Nelson and I have planned a surprise picnic in honor of Sarah's birthday this afternoon. You and your helper are more than welcome to join us if you have no other plans."

"I have no plans, and I'd like to come, but I'm not sure about Ned. He's not very social, but I will check with him and see."

"Great. The picnic's going to be on the grassy area outside our store. We'll start eating around one, or as soon as everyone we've invited gets there."

"That sounds fine. It'll give me time to speak with Ned, and then I'll be over to join you." Elias started to move away, but halted and turned to face her again. "Is there anything I can bring?"

She shook her head. "Just a hearty appetite. There's always lots of good food at one of our picnics."

"All right then. I'll see you around one."

Elias moved over to where the pastor and his wife stood, greeting people near the door, and waited his turn. After he'd spoken to Betsy and told her how much he'd enjoyed the music, he shook Pastor William's hand. "I enjoyed the service. The music and sermon were both uplifting."

"This is a hand-clapping congregation." Pastor William smiled. "It took me awhile to adjust to that when I first came to pastor the church, but now I can't imagine being anywhere but here with these warm, friendly folks."

"I know what you mean," Elias said. "The services in the church where I grew up are very formal. No one would dare to shout *amen* or clap their hands."

"Starting next week, after the morning service, I'll be holding regular services along the canal near the lock tender's house. Now I have to say that those services really bring out the people's enthusiasm."

"I assume the services along the canal are for the benefit of the boatmen who might not feel comfortable inside a church?"

The pastor nodded. "My wife's father used to hold services along the canal, and I continued the tradition at Betsy's suggestion." He smiled. "Many a boatman's been won to the Lord after attending one of our canal services."

Maybe there's some hope for Ned, Elias thought. "Perhaps I can talk my helper into attending one of your canal services with me when we're in the area again."

"That would be nice. I'm sure if nothing else he'd enjoy hearing my wife play her zither. Some of the boatmen who play instruments often join in, too."

"I play the accordion," Elias said. "Do you think folks would enjoy hearing that?"

"Oh, definitely. That would be a nice addition to our services, so do bring it if you come, and even here at the church, we'd enjoy hearing you play sometime."

Elias smiled. Not only was there some hope for Ned, but now he'd have the chance to play his accordion in praise to the Lord. He could hardly wait for the next time he was in Walnutport on a Sunday. Maybe he'd plan their trips in such a way that he could be here most every Sunday.

Chapter 15

As Patrick O'Grady stood near Sarah, watching her open the birthday presents some folks had brought to the picnic, he found himself hoping she would like the box of chocolates he'd bought for her and that she'd eventually agree to become his wife. Patrick had never admitted it to anyone, but he'd been interested in Sarah when they were children. From the first day Sarah had come into Pop's blacksmith shop with her daddy, Patrick had been intrigued—not only by her pretty face, but by her determination and spirited ways.

When Sarah became a teenager, he'd found her even more appealing, but she hadn't returned his interest, choosing instead to run off with Sam Turner, who was even more spirited than Sarah. Patrick always wondered if Sarah had chosen Sam over him because Sam was determined to get away from the canal, while Patrick was content to stay and take over his father's blacksmith shop.

He'd known from the comments Sarah had made that she would have done most anything to get away from the canal. Yet here she was, not only living along the canal, but doing the job of a man.

If she married me, Patrick thought as he gazed at Sarah's pretty face, *she wouldn't have to work anymore, and I'd have a wife to come home to at night, not to mention someone who'd be there to clean the house and put decent meals on the table.*

He glanced over at Sarah's oldest boy, Sammy, and grimaced. The only drawback to marrying Sarah would be in having to help her raise those three children—and one of them thought he was too big for his britches.

Oh well, I'll worry about that when the time comes. The first thing I need to do is win Sarah's heart. Maybe I should consider going to church so I can see her more often, and then she might see me in a different light.

Tears sprang to Sarah's eyes as she was handed several gifts. Just the picnic in honor of her birthday was surprise enough, and she'd certainly never expected so many people would come and give her birthday presents. She'd already opened a box filled with sweet-smelling soaps from Betsy and Pastor William, as well as a journal that Sammy's schoolteacher had given her.

"This one's from us," Kelly said, handing Sarah a large, flat package.

The first thing Sarah saw when she tore off the wrapping paper was some pale blue material.

"It's for a new dress," Kelly explained. "I know you don't have time to sew, but I thought I'd take the material to Doris Brown from church, who has recently begun doing some sewing for others, and then she can make the dress for you."

"I appreciate that." Sarah only had one Sunday dress, so it would be nice to have another.

"The gift that's under the material is just from me," Kelly said.

Sarah lifted the material and a sob rose in her throat as she gazed at a beautiful painting of her three children playing in the grassy area in front of her house. Behind them, several ducks floated on the canal.

"This is so nice," Sarah murmured. "Thank you, Kelly."

"You're welcome."

"Open mine next," Sammy said, pushing a paper sack in Sarah's direction.

She opened the sack and withdrew a calico sunbonnet with dark blue trim.

"Your old bonnet's lookin' pretty shabby," Sammy said, "so I bought ya a new one with the money I earned leadin' Elias's mules."

"Thank you, son, I appreciate that." Sarah pulled Sammy close and gave him a hug. It touched her to know that even though she'd disciplined him yesterday, he'd spent his hard-earned money on a gift for her.

"I have a present for you, too." Patrick handed her a small rectangular box wrapped in fancy red paper.

Sarah pulled the paper away and lifted the lid on the box. She smiled when she saw the box of chocolates inside. Candy, especially fancy chocolates, was a luxury—something she never bought for herself, so this was a real treat.

"They each have a different filling," Patrick said, looking rather pleased with himself.

She smiled. "Thank you. I appreciate the gift and will enjoy every bite."

Willis tugged on Sarah's sleeve. "Ain't ya gonna give us any of them chocolates, Mama?"

She tweaked his nose. "If you're a good boy, I'll be happy to share."

He grinned as he bobbed his head. "I'll be good as gold; I promise."

Everyone chuckled, and then Mike stepped forward and said, "Now it's time to eat the birthday cake, but before we do that, there's a song that I know from a reliable source"—he smiled at Kelly—"was a special favorite of your mama's. We'd like to sing it for you, Sarah." He motioned to Elias, who stood nearby. "When I talked to Elias after church, I found out that he plays the accordion, so I asked him to accompany us as we sing 'What a Friend We Have in Jesus.' "

Elias played a few introductory notes, and then everyone began to sing: *"What a friend we have in Jesus, all our sins and griefs to bear! What a privilege to carry everything to God in prayer!"*

Sarah's eyes clouded with tears, and she blinked a couple of times to keep them from spilling over. It was wonderful to know that she had so many caring friends.

"Thank you, everyone," she said when the singing ended and she could trust her voice. "This has been a very special birthday."

"Why don't we sing a few more hymns now?" Ben Hanson, one of their church deacons, suggested.

Pastor William looked over at Elias. "Would you be willing to accompany us?"

Elias nodded. "I know most of the traditional hymns, so I'd be happy to play along."

For the next hour, everyone sat on the grass and sang a variety of hymns. The singing probably would have continued for another hour or so, but the sky had darkened, and it began to rain.

In short order, all the leftover dishes, as well as Sarah's presents, were gathered up, and everyone started for home.

"Thanks for making my day so special," Sarah said, giving Kelly a hug.

"You're very welcome."

As the raindrops increased, Sarah urged her children to hurry home.

"Aw, do we hafta go now?" Sammy frowned. "I wanna visit with Elias awhile."

"I'd like to visit with you, too," Elias said, "but we'll see each other again—maybe the next time I come through the lock."

"Okay." Sammy turned and started running toward home, singing loudly as he went: *"I've got a mule, she's such a fool, she never pays me no heed. I'll build a fire beneath her tail, and then she'll show me some speed!"*

Sarah clenched her teeth. It was nice to see Sammy so happy, but she didn't want him singing or even thinking about things related to the canal, fearful that he might want to drop out of school and become a mule driver. Sarah didn't know what she'd do if that happened. She really did need to find some way to get her children away from the canal.

Chapter 16

*I*t had been two weeks since Sarah's surprise birthday picnic, and every time Sarah looked at the picture Kelly had drawn of her children, which she'd hung in the parlor, she thanked God for the privilege of being their mother. Even though she didn't get to spend nearly as much time as she'd like with them, she enjoyed every free moment they could be together.

This morning, as she slipped her new bonnet onto her head, she appreciated once again the thoughtfulness of her oldest boy. He was a lot like his father—headstrong, determined, and much too outspoken, but he had a tender spirit and wanted to please.

School would be out for the summer in just a few weeks, and Sarah knew that Sammy would do his best to help wherever he could. Of course there were many things he couldn't do well, especially cooking. However, with Betsy's help, most of their meals were taken care of, and for that, Sarah felt grateful. Betsy was also good with Sarah's children, often finding fun things for them to do and keeping a close eye on them whenever they went outside to play. What a shame that Betsy didn't have any children of her own.

Sarah glanced at the jars of jelly stacked in her pantry and thought of Maria. She'd gotten a letter from Roger's wife yesterday, letting her know how Maria was doing. She'd been seeing a specialist in Easton but was told there wasn't much that could be done. Her eyes were getting progressively worse. Sarah was glad Maria was where she could be looked after. She'd done well by the children for many months, but now it was her turn to be the one who was cared for.

Sarah pulled her thoughts aside and looked at

her children, who still sat at the kitchen table, eating their breakfast. "I'm going outside to hang out the wash. Sammy, as soon as you're done eating, you need to get ready for school."

"Okay, Mama."

Sarah picked up her laundry basket and opened the door. As she stepped outside, a blast of muggy, warm air hit her full in the face. If it was this warm in late May, she could only imagine how hot it would be by the middle of summer.

Sarah set the wicker basket under the clothesline and had just hung the first towel in place when she heard a conch shell blowing in the distance. She knew it would be several minutes before the boat showed up so she hurried to hang a few more pieces of laundry.

When the boat finally appeared, she left the clothes and hurried to the lock. The boat's captain, Lars Olsen, gave her a friendly wave. "Got any bread today, Sarah? I could use a loaf or two."

"I have some in the house. I'll get it for you as soon as your boat's gone through the lock."

"All right then. I'll tie up on the other side after we've passed through."

Sarah pulled the pin out of the wicket, being careful not to let it slip. She didn't want to fall again and reinjure her ribs—or worse yet, end up with a more serious injury.

Once Lars's boat was through, Sarah dashed into the house and got two loaves of bread. She frowned when she saw that the children were still at the table.

"Hurry up, Sammy. You're going to be late for school if you don't get a move on."

His nose wrinkled. "Wish I didn't hafta go. Wish I could stay home and do some fishin' in the canal."

"If and when you're allowed to go fishing, it'll probably be during the summer when you're out of school, and it will definitely have to be with an adult."

"Elias said he might take me fishin' sometime, and he's an adult."

"We'll have to wait and see how it goes. Elias isn't usually here long enough to do any fishing."

"If he's here on a Sunday he could."

She thumped his shoulder lightly. "Maybe so, but right now you need to get ready for school, and I need to get this bread out to Lars."

Sarah hurried out the door and over to where Lars had docked his boat.

"Thanks, Sarah," he said when she handed him the loaf of bread. He gave her the money he owed and stepped back onto his boat. "I'll see you again on my way back from Mauch Chunk."

Sarah put the money in her apron pocket and returned to her job of hanging out the wash. She'd only been working a few minutes when Sammy came out the door with his lunch pail.

"I'm headin' to school now, Mama."

"Okay, have a good day."

He waved and hurried off in the direction of the schoolhouse.

A few minutes later, Betsy showed up, wearing a smile that stretched ear to ear.

"You're looking mighty chipper on this hot humid morning," Sarah said, wiping the perspiration from her forehead.

"Actually, I'm not feeling that chipper, but I am deliriously happy," Betsy said, stepping up to Sarah.

"How come?"

"I went to see Dr. McGrath yesterday, and what I've suspected for the last few weeks is true."

"What's that?"

Betsy's smile widened. "I'm in a family way. The baby should be born sometime in December."

Sarah dropped Sammy's wet trousers into the basket and gave Betsy a hug. "I'm so happy for you. I was just thinking this morning that you'd make a good mother."

Betsy sighed. "Oh, I hope so. I didn't always have a fondness for children, but that all changed during the time I spent helping at the orphanage in New York. I've had a desire ever since to have children of my own."

"I'm sure you and William will make good parents. He seems to have a way with kids, too."

"Yes, he does, and he was so happy when we learned that I'm expecting. In fact, he can't quit talking about it, and has already begun thinking of names for the baby."

Sarah chuckled. "Sam did that when I was pregnant with Sammy. When we couldn't make a decision, we finally decided to call the baby Sam Jr. if it was a boy."

"William said that if our baby's a boy he doesn't want to name it after himself. He said William Covington IV would be a bit too much."

Sarah smiled. "You could always call him Willy."

"Oh sure, and then with your Willis and our Willy, everyone would be confused."

"Well, maybe it'll be a girl, and then you can call her Betsy."

"No way. One Betsy in the family's enough. If it's a girl, I think we might name her Rebekah. I've always liked that name, and we can call her Becky for short."

"So how are you?" Sarah asked. "You said you're not feeling chipper. Does that mean you're not feeling well?"

Betsy nodded slowly. "My stomach's been real queasy, especially in the mornings, which I realize now is because I'm pregnant. I also tire easily."

"Maybe you should be at home resting instead of coming over here to help me every day." Sarah slipped her arm around Betsy's waist. "I don't want you to feel obligated to help just because you said you would. Things have changed, and your health and the health of your baby should come first."

"But you need someone's help here. Taking care of the lock, watching the children, baking bread, and keeping house—it's all too much for one person to do alone."

"I'll manage somehow. Sammy will be out of school soon, and he'll help me as much as he can."

Betsy bent down and picked up one of Helen's little gingham dresses. "Let's just wait and see how I feel in the days ahead, okay?"

Sarah nodded. "But I want you to promise that if you need to quit you'll say so."

"I promise."

As Patrick approached the lock tender's house, he spotted Sarah and Betsy standing near the clothesline, and his heartbeat picked up speed. Sarah's long dark hair hung down her back in gentle waves, and the floppy sunbonnet her son had given her was perched on her head. Despite the fact that she wore a faded yellow dress that was obviously well-worn, he thought she looked beautiful. He wished Betsy wasn't here so he could talk to Sarah in private, but he hoped that once he approached them Betsy would go inside.

"Top of the morning to you," Patrick said, stepping between the two women and smiling at Sarah. "Sure is a nice day, wouldn't ya say?"

She gave a nod. "I just wish it wasn't so warm and muggy."

"It's that, all right." He gave Betsy a slight nod. "Did ya come to help Sarah again today?"

"Yes, I sure did, and I'd better get inside and see how the children are doing. It was nice seeing you, Patrick." Betsy turned and headed for the house.

"Came to see if you have any bread," Patrick said, moving closer to Sarah.

"Yes, I made some last night. I'll go get a loaf from the kitchen." Sarah turned toward the house.

"I'll go with you." Patrick hurried along beside her. "I also came by to see if there's anything you'd like me to do while I'm here."

"That's kind of you, but I can't think of anything right now."

Sarah opened the door to the house, and as they stepped into the kitchen, Patrick was greeted by a yappy little dog.

Woof! Woof! Woof! The wiry terrier bared its teeth and snapped at Patrick's pant leg.

"Bristle Face, no!" Sarah pointed to the braided throw rug in front of the sink. "Go lie down!"

The dog slunk off to the rug, growling all the way.

"Sorry about that. I don't know what's wrong with him this morning. He's usually friendly to everyone and rarely ever growls."

"He don't like everyone, Mama," Willis said as

116

he and his little sister entered the room. "Some folks he don't like a'tall—same as me. I don't like everyone neither."

Patrick gritted his teeth. *That boy is sure rude. I bet all three of Sarah's kids are probably too much for her to handle. I think what they need is a father who can teach them some manners.*

Sarah shook her finger at Willis. "That's not a nice way to talk, son. You shouldn't dislike anyone."

"Sorry," Willis mumbled.

Sarah turned to face Patrick. "How many loaves of bread did you want?"

"Just one for now. When I run out, I'll be back for more." Patrick looked over at the children, wishing they'd go back to wherever they'd been before he came into the house with Sarah. "What'd you two have for breakfast this morning?" he asked when he noticed a blob of something stuck to Helen's dress.

"We had mush," Willis answered.

"We had mush," Helen echoed.

Patrick wrinkled his nose. "I've never cared much for mush, unless it's covered in maple syrup."

"We can't afford maple syrup," Sarah said. "We use melted brown sugar instead."

"Maybe I'll bring you some maple syrup sometime."

"There's no need for that. My kids are fine using

brown sugar." Sarah handed Patrick a loaf of bread. "Here you go."

Patrick paid Sarah. "Thanks a lot. I'm sure it's real tasty bread."

"I hope you'll excuse me, but I need to get the rest of my laundry hung out, and then I have some other chores to do when I'm not letting boats through the lock."

Patrick was tempted to hang around while Sarah did her chores but figured she might not appreciate it. Besides, he had some things of his own to get done at the blacksmith shop. So he picked up the bread and headed for the door. "I'll see you soon, Sarah," he called over his shoulder.

"Sure will be glad when we get to Walnutport," Ned said, joining Elias at the bow of the boat. "I'm just about outa chewin' tobacco, and I'm hopin' you'll stop at Cooper's store so I can get some more."

Elias frowned. "Chewing's a nasty habit, Ned. You should give it up and spend your money on something more constructive."

"Can't think of nothin' I'd rather spend my money on. Unless maybe it's for a bottle of whiskey."

"Whiskey's a tool of the devil. It'll take you down, sure thing."

Ned shrugged his shoulders. "It's my life, and I'll go down any way I choose."

"I know it's your life, but the Bible says—"

"Don't care what the Bible says and don't need ya preachin' to me neither."

"I didn't mean it as preaching, I just wanted you to—"

"Whoa! Whoa there!" Bobby shouted.

"What's wrong?" Elias turned his attention to the towpath. "Oh no, one of the mules is down." He steered the boat toward shore.

"Daisy stepped in a rut, and I think her leg's broken," Bobby said, eyes wide with obvious concern. "I can see the bone stickin' out."

"Now that's just great," Ned mumbled. "The last thing we need is a dead mule."

"She's not dead," Elias said. "Bobby said he thinks she's broken her leg."

Ned slowly shook his head. "We can't fix her leg."

Daisy kept braying and trying to get up. Elias wished there was something he could do to help the poor mule.

"Look, boss, the critter has to be put out of her misery. Now I'm goin' below to get my gun."

Elias stood there in stunned silence. With only one mule, they'd never get to Mauch Chunk for another load of coal. They'd have to stop in Walnutport for sure now and see if they could find another mule.

Chapter 17

That afternoon, Elias's boat limped into Walnutport with only one mule pulling for all she was worth. While Elias and Ned went to speak with Mike Cooper about getting another mule, Bobby stayed outside to keep an eye on the boat and feed and water Dolly.

Entering Cooper's store, Elias spotted Mike behind the counter, waiting on Bart Jarmon, a burly boatman. Elias held back and waited until Bart had exited the store, then he stepped up to the counter.

"It's good to see you again," Mike said. "What can I help you with?"

"I need a new mule and was hoping you might know where I can find one."

Mike's eyebrows rose. "What do you need a mule for? I thought you had two good ones."

"I did, but one of them stepped in a hole and broke her leg. Ned had to put her down."

"Sorry to hear that." Mike fingered his mustache. "Let's see now. . . . I think Patrick O'Grady, the town's blacksmith, traded some of his work for a mule awhile back."

"Maybe I'll head over there."

Elias found Ned at the back of the store, no doubt in search of his chewing tobacco. "Mike says the blacksmith has a mule he might be willing to sell, so I'm going over to his shop and see if he's there."

Ned gave a nod. "Sure, go right ahead. I'll get what I'm needin' here and wait for ya at the boat."

"Hopefully I won't be too long." Elias turned and headed out the door.

Patrick had just finished putting new shoes on the doctor's horse when that fancy-talking boatman with the red blotch on his face showed up.

"I lost one of my mules, and Mike Cooper mentioned that you might have one I could buy," Elias said, stepping up to Patrick.

Patrick nodded. "I do have a mule. Somebody who couldn't pay for my services gave her to me a few weeks ago. Not sure what I'm gonna do with her, though. So if you're interested you can have her for fifty dollars."

Elias scratched the side of his head. "Guess that's a fair enough price."

"I think so, since a lot of mules go for as much as seventy-five dollars."

"Has your mule ever pulled a canal boat?"

"Sure thing. Least that's what her owner said when he gave her to me."

"Okay, good." Elias reached into his pants pocket and pulled out the money, which he handed to Patrick. "Guess I'd better get the mule and be on my way, because I want to make a quick stop to see Sammy Turner."

Patrick's eyebrows lifted. "Sarah's son?"

"Uh-huh. The boy led my mules while my helper, Ned, was tending the lock for Sarah after she fell and hurt her ribs."

"I heard about that. Ever since Sarah's husband died, she's been real protective of her kids. I was surprised she'd allow Sammy to go with you."

Elias leaned against Patrick's workbench. "Well, she didn't exactly say he could go. Sammy took off without her permission."

"I'm sure she was upset about that."

"She was at first, but Sarah seems to be an understanding woman, and after I apologized and explained everything, she was quite nice about it."

Patrick studied Elias several seconds. From the look he saw on Elias's face when he'd mentioned Sarah's name it made him wonder if the man might be interested in her.

"I've known Sarah since we were kids," Patrick said. "I'd have to say that she and I are good friends."

"I see." Elias turned toward the door of Patrick's shop. "Well, I'd best get that mule."

"Sure, of course." As Patrick led the way to the stall where he'd put the mule, he wondered if the boatman was using Sammy to get close to Sarah. *Well, if he is, I'd better move fast.*

• • •

"I see ya got yourself a new mule," Ned said when Elias returned to the boat.

Elias ground his teeth together. "Yes, and I've already discovered that she's got a mind of her own. The stubborn animal balked every step of the way."

"Did Patrick say the mule was used to pullin' a boat?"

Elias nodded. "But I guess that doesn't mean she can't be stubborn."

"Well, hopefully she'll do better once she's harnessed up. Since Dolly's the lead mule, I'm sure she'll show this new one who's boss. What's the mule's name, anyway?"

"I don't know. Guess we could call her Wilma, since she's so willful."

Ned scratched the mule behind her ears. "All right then, Wilma, let's get you harnessed and ready to go."

"Before we head out, I want to go over to the lock tender's house and see Sammy," Elias said.

Ned frowned. "For cryin' out loud! We've lost enough time already! If you get involved talkin' to that kid, we'll never get to Mauch Chunk."

Irritation welled in Elias. It seemed like Ned was forever telling him what to do. "I won't be over there that long. I just want to see how Sammy's doing, and then we can get through the lock and be on our way."

"You sure it's Sammy you're wantin' to see and not his purty mama?"

Elias shook his head. "I'm only interested in Sarah's son."

"Whatever you say. After all, I'm just a dumb helper, and you're the educated boss."

Choosing to ignore Ned's snide remark, Elias turned Wilma over to his outspoken helper and walked away.

When he arrived at Sarah's, her three children were playing with their dog on the grassy area along the side of the house. As soon as Sammy spotted Elias, he raced right over to him. "Sure is good to see ya again! Can ya stay awhile and visit?"

Elias shook his head. "I'm afraid not. I just wanted to stop and say hello and see how you're doing."

Sammy grinned up at him. "I'm fine, but I'll be doin' even better after school's out for the summer."

"When will that be?"

"Tomorrow's our last day."

"I'll bet you're looking forward to being home all summer."

"Sure am." Sammy tipped his head and shielded his eyes from the glare of the sun. "Can we still go fishin' sometime?"

"I'm planning on it. Thought maybe we could go when I'm in the area on a Sunday again. It'll be after church, of course."

"That sounds good, but I'll have to ask Mama first." Sammy's forehead creased. "Sure wouldn't wanna upset her the way I did when I led the mules for ya."

"No, we surely wouldn't want to do that." Elias glanced at the house. "Where is your mother, Sammy? Is she inside?"

Sammy nodded. "She's bakin' more bread to sell to the boatmen."

Elias was tempted to knock on the door and say hello to Sarah, but when he glanced over his shoulder and saw Ned and Bobby waiting at the boat, he changed his mind. "I'd better get going," he told Sammy, "but I'll see you again soon, I promise."

Chapter 18

*T*wo weeks later, Pastor William showed up at Sarah's, explaining that Betsy wasn't feeling well and didn't think she could help Sarah today.

"I'm sorry to hear that. Has her morning sickness gotten worse?" Sarah asked.

He nodded. "She's very tired, too, and the doctor recommended that she stay home and rest."

"That's probably what she needs to do then."

"I'd stay and help you today, but I think I need to be at home in case Betsy needs me for anything."

"You're right; your place is with her. Since

Sammy's out of school now, I think with his help we can manage."

"Are you sure? Maybe I can find one of the ladies from church who'd be willing to fill in for Betsy."

"No, that's okay. We'll be fine."

"All right then. I'll be on my way." Pastor William smiled and went out the door.

Sarah sighed, wondering how things would really go with just Sammy's help today. Maybe she should have taken Pastor William up on his offer to find someone else.

For the past two weeks, Elias's boat had been moving up and down the canal at a snail's pace, thanks to the contrite mule he'd bought from Patrick O'Grady. The stubborn critter kept nipping at Dolly, tried to kick Bobby a couple of times, and stopped right in her tracks whenever she didn't like something she saw. Elias had hoped to stop in Walnutport so he could go to church there, and hopefully take Sammy fishing, but so far it hadn't worked out for him to be in that area on a Sunday. If Wilma didn't start acting right he might have to sell her and invest in another mule—one that would cooperate so they could make better time.

On the brighter side, Elias had gotten word from his sister, Carolyn, who was a teacher in Easton. She'd surprised him by saying that she wanted to spend her summer break on his boat, and that she'd be glad to do the cooking, cleaning, and laundry for Elias and his helpers. That meant Ned could take over for Elias at the tiller more often, giving Elias a break.

Today, when Elias stopped in Easton to deliver his load of coal, he would pick up Carolyn. Of course, Carolyn's letter had mentioned that Mother and Father weren't too happy about her joining him for the summer. However, Carolyn had a mind of her own, so probably nothing their parents said had made much difference to her.

"You'd better quit daydreamin' and watch where you're steerin' the boat," Ned said, nudging Elias's arm. "If you're not careful you'll run us aground."

"I was just thinking about my sister, who'll be joining us soon."

Ned snorted. "Just what we need—some hoity-toity woman on the boat tellin' us what to do."

"Carolyn's not hoity-toity. She's pleasant, smart, and I think she's a pretty good cook."

"You sayin' I'm a bad cook? Is that what you're sayin', boss?"

"I'm not saying that at all." Elias bumped Ned's arm this time. "Just think, if you don't have to cook you'll have more time for other things. Maybe you can get that stubborn Wilma trained to pull a little better, and then we'll be able to travel faster, which means we'll make more money."

Ned puckered his lips. "You mean *you'll* make more money, don'tcha? You're the captain of this boat, not me."

Elias merely shrugged. At least Ned hadn't called him *the boss* again.

As Sarah's day progressed, things went from bad to worse. She'd been trying to bake bread all day, but between the boats coming through the lock, and the children vying for her attention, by midafternoon she still had not made any bread. This wasn't good, because she only had a few loaves left, and if any of the boatmen stopped and bought bread today she'd be out.

Wo–o–o–o! Wo–o–o–o! Wo–o–o–o! Wo–o–o–o! The moaning of a conch shell, and then another, alerted her that two boats were coming. Maybe after they'd passed through the lock, she'd have time to make some bread.

"I've got to go! Keep an eye on your sister and brother," Sarah called to Sammy as she raced out the door.

Sarah let the first boat through, and then the second.

Wo–o–o–o! Wo–o–o–o! Another boat rounded the bend.

She'd just begun to raise the lock again, when Sammy raced out the door wearing a panicked expression. "Helen's gone! I can't find her anywhere!"

Chapter 19

Sarah quickly let the boat through the lock and dashed into the house behind Sammy. "Where'd you last see your sister?" she panted.

He shrugged. "I ain't really sure."

"What do you mean? Weren't you watching her like I told you to do?"

"I was, but you know how Helen is, Mama. She moves around all over the place. I can't be watchin' her and Willis at the same time."

"You can if you keep them in the same room with you." Sarah cupped her hands around her mouth. "Helen! Where are you?"

"She ain't in here, Mama," Willis said when Sarah stepped into the kitchen. "She ain't anywhere in the house."

"How do you know?"

"'Cause Sammy and I went lookin'."

"That's right," Sammy put in. "We looked everywhere down here and upstairs, too."

"Did you see her go outside?"

Sammy shook his head. "But she mighta snuck out when we wasn't lookin'."

Sarah's mouth went dry, and her heart began to pound. If Helen went outside by herself, she could have fallen in the canal. *Oh dear Lord, please let her be all right.*

She drew in a deep breath and tried to think.

"Where's Bristle Face? He usually follows Helen wherever she goes."

Sammy turned his hands palms up. "Beats me. Haven't seen him for quite a spell neither."

Another conch shell blew, and Sarah groaned. She needed to let the boat through the lock, but she needed to find Helen more than anything. Oh, how she wished Betsy was here to help her right now.

"Sammy, run down to the store and get Uncle Mike. Tell him that Helen's missing, and that I've gone looking for her. Ask if he can leave the store long enough to come and let the boat through the lock."

"I can do it, Mama. I can let the boat through the lock," Sammy said.

Sarah shook her head. "No, you can't. It's too hard for you, and you might get hurt. Just do as I said and go get Uncle Mike."

Sammy had just started across the room, when the door swung open and Kelly stepped in with Helen and Bristle Face. "Are you missing someone here?" she asked, looking at Sarah.

Sarah's breath caught in her throat, and she bent down and swept Helen into her arms. "Oh, I was so worried. Where were these two?" she asked, looking at Kelly.

"Came over to our store. Helen said she was takin' Bristle Face for a walk, and I figured she'd wandered off without your permission."

Sarah nodded, feeling such relief. "I thought we could get along okay with just Sammy's help today, but apparently I was wrong."

"What do you mean? Where's Betsy?" Kelly asked.

"She's not feeling well, so she stayed home today."

Wo–o–o–o! Wo–o–o–o!

"The boat's getting closer; I've got to go. Can you stay and watch the kids while I open the lock?" Sarah asked her sister.

Kelly nodded. "Of course; and as soon as you're done, I'll take your kids to stay at my place for the rest of the day."

"Thank you," Sarah said with a nod. It might not be the best situation, since Kelly had her hands full watching her own two children, plus helping Mike in the store, but at least Sarah would be able to get some baking done when she wasn't busy opening the lock.

"How are you feeling?" William asked Betsy the following morning when he stepped into the kitchen.

She leaned against the cupboard and heaved a sigh. "About the same. I had no idea being pregnant could make a person feel so sick and tired."

"Dr. McGrath said that it's different with everyone." William gave Betsy a hug. "You're just one of the unfortunate women who feels sicker than some. I'm sure it'll get better, but in the meantime, I want you to rest as much as possible and drink that ginger tea the doctor suggested."

"But I didn't go to Sarah's yesterday to help out, and I really should go there today."

"No, you need to stay home and rest."

"I'm worried about Sarah. How's she going to manage with just Sammy's help? He's only a little boy."

William slipped his arms around Betsy and kissed the top of her head. "You let me worry about that. As soon as I've had some breakfast, I'm going out to look for someone to help Sarah."

Sarah had just finished the breakfast dishes when a knock sounded on the door.

Woof! Woof! Bristle Face, who'd been sleeping on the braided throw rug in front of the stove, leaped up and raced to the door.

Sarah gently pushed the dog aside and opened the door. She was surprised to see Pastor William there with Ruby Miller, one of the older women who attended their church.

"Good morning, Sarah," he said with a cheerful smile. "I knew it must have been hard for you yesterday, so I brought Ruby to help you today."

Sarah wasn't sure if the elderly woman could keep up with three lively children, but she smiled at Ruby and said, "I appreciate you coming."

Ruby gave a nod. "I'm sure the children and I will get along well."

Sarah turned to Pastor William. "Give Betsy my love and tell her to keep getting lots of rest."

"I will." He nodded at Ruby. "I'll be back to get you this evening."

Pastor William had just gone out the door when a conch shell sounded, followed by another and another. "The children have already had their breakfast," Sarah told Ruby, "but if you could see that the kitchen gets cleaned up and make sure the children get dressed while I'm letting those boats through the lock, I'd appreciate it."

"No problem." Ruby waved a hand. "You go ahead and take care of business. By the time you come back, the kitchen will be clean as a whistle."

When Sarah stepped outside, she saw three boats waiting in line to go through the lock. She was glad to have some help in the house today, because if the boats kept coming like this all day, she'd have her hands full just opening and closing the lock.

After the boats had gone through, Sarah turned toward the house. She was almost to the door when another conch shell sounded. By the time she'd let that boat through another boat was coming.

It was nearly noon by the time Sarah had a break and could return to the house. When she stepped into the kitchen she expected to see Ruby fixing lunch. What she saw instead caused her to gasp.

Helen sat on the kitchen floor with an open bag of flour in front of her. Some had spilled onto the floor, but most of it was in her hair, on her dress, and all over her arms and legs.

"Oh no—not the flour again," Sarah moaned.

Willis sat at the kitchen table eating a piece of bread that he'd smeared with strawberry jam, but there was no sign of Sammy or Ruby.

Sarah placed her hand on Willis's head. "Where's Sammy?"

"He took Bristle Face out for a walk."

"Where's Ruby?"

"She's in the parlor takin' a nap."

Sarah frowned. So much for the help she thought she was getting today. She'd have been better off with no help at all!

She cleaned up Helen and the floury mess, then hurried into the parlor. Sure enough, Ruby was sprawled out on the sofa, her eyes shut, her mouth hanging slightly open.

Sarah bent down and gently shook the woman's shoulders.

Ruby's eyes snapped open. "Oh, Sarah, it's you! Guess I must have dozed off."

Sarah didn't bother to tell Ruby about the mess she'd found in the kitchen. Instead, she helped the exhausted-looking woman to her feet. "It's noon. If you feel rested enough would you please fix the children some lunch?"

Ruby yawned noisily. "Of course." She ambled into the kitchen just as another conch shell blew.

Sarah could only hope that by the time she returned to the house, the children's lunch would be made and Sammy would be back from walking the dog.

Chapter 20

*W*hen Sarah awoke the following morning, she had a pounding headache. Oh, how she wished she could stay in bed and sleep all day. But duty called, and already, at just a few minutes after five, a conch shell was blowing.

Sarah hurried to get dressed and tiptoed down the stairs so she wouldn't wake the children. Amazingly enough, the blowing of the conch shells didn't usually wake them, but if Sarah moved about the house too loudly, they were wide awake.

The conch shell blew again, and Sarah stepped outside just in time to see Bart Jarmon's boat approach the lock. Bart was not her favorite person—especially not this early in the morning when she hadn't even had a cup of coffee yet. She hoped he wouldn't make any rude remarks, like he'd often done in the past. He'd have never done that when Sam was alive, because Bart, along with all the other canalers, respected Sam and knew better than to smart off to him the way some of them did to Sarah.

As Sarah prepared to open the lock she prayed that God would give her the right words, should Bart say anything crude. She was relieved when his only remark was, "It's already gettin' warm. Looks like it's gonna be another hot one today."

Sarah nodded and called, "Summer's here. There's no doubt about it."

"Yep."

She stood silently while the water level rose and was relieved when Bart's boat was on its way. She hurried back to the house to start breakfast.

By the time Sarah had some bacon and eggs cooking, the children were up.

"Somethin' sure smells good, Mama," Willis said. "I'm hungry!"

Sarah smiled. "If the three of you will take a seat at the table, I'll dish up your breakfast."

The children clambered onto their chairs with eager expressions.

"Sure don't understand why I haven't seen Elias lately," Sammy said. "Makes me wonder if he'll ever take me fishin'."

"The last time he came through the lock, he was having trouble with his new mule," Sarah said, placing a platter of eggs and bacon on the table. "Maybe the mule's still acting up, and that's slowing him down."

Sammy's forehead creased. "If I was leadin' his mules, bet I could make that stubborn mule go faster."

Sarah frowned. "Don't get any ideas about leading Elias's mules, because that's not going to happen ever again."

"But Mama, I could make us some extra money."

Sarah shook her head. "We don't need extra money that bad, and I won't have any of my children walking the dusty towpath from sunup to sunset." She placed an egg and a hunk of bacon on Sammy's plate. "Now please stop talking and eat your breakfast."

Sarah dished up an egg and some bacon for Helen and Willis, as well as some for herself. She'd just started eating when a knock sounded on the door. "That must be Ruby," she told the children. "You need to help her out today and not make any messes."

Sarah hurried to the door, and when she opened it she was surprised to see Hortence Andrews, one of the young, single women from church, standing on the porch. "I'm here to help out," she said. "Pastor William came by my house last night and said that Ruby didn't feel up to coming anymore, so I'll be helping you from now on."

Sarah heaved a sigh of relief. Surely things would go better today with someone younger and more energetic overseeing the children.

"I'm anxious to introduce you to the storekeeper and his wife," Elias told his sister as his boat approached Cooper's store. "They're good Christian people, and I think you'll like them as much as I do."

Carolyn smiled, and her blue eyes twinkled as the sunlight brought out the golden color of her shiny blond hair, which she'd worn in a loose bun. "I'm sure if you like them, then I will, too."

"Elias likes everyone," Ned said with a grunt. "Never met anyone, 'cept for his grandpa, who was as agreeable as him."

Elias's face heated. "I'm only trying to be a good Christian."

Ned folded his arms. "Humph! I've known a lot of nice folks who weren't Christians, and I've known some who called themselves Christians but acted as disagreeable as that stupid, stubborn mule you bought from the blacksmith."

Elias made no comment. He wasn't looking for an argument with Ned this morning.

When they docked at the store, Ned put down the gangplank and Elias helped Carolyn off the boat. "Are you coming into the store with us?" he called over his shoulder to Ned.

"Nope, not today. I'm gonna sit right here and have myself a smoke."

Carolyn wrinkled her nose but said nothing.

Elias grimaced. He wished Ned would give up his nasty habits.

"You can unhitch the mules and tie them to a tree so they can rest awhile," Elias told Bobby. He handed the boy a quarter. "Then you can go into the store and get yourself some candy or something cold to drink."

Bobby's eyes lit up. "With a whole quarter I can buy both!"

Elias smiled and patted the boy's shoulder. "You work hard and deserve a special treat."

When they entered the store, Elias led Carolyn over to the counter and introduced her to Mike.

"It's nice to meet you," Mike said, shaking Carolyn's hand. "Elias mentioned that you'd be joining him on the boat for the summer."

Carolyn smiled. "I've been looking forward to it."

Elias glanced around. "Where's your wife? I'd like her to meet Carolyn, too."

Mike motioned to the adjoining room. "She's in her art gallery working on a new painting."

"I'd like to see it," Carolyn said. "Would she mind if I went in?"

Mike shook his head. "Not at all. Kelly never minds when someone watches her paint."

Elias led the way to Kelly's little studio. They found her standing in front of a wooden easel painting a picture of a beautiful rainbow hovering over the canal.

Kelly smiled as they approached her. "It's nice to see you again, Elias."

"It's good to see you, too." He motioned to Carolyn. "This is my sister, Carolyn."

Kelly wiped her hands on her apron and extended one hand to Carolyn. "It's real nice to meet you."

"It's good to meet you as well." Carolyn moved closer to Kelly's easel. "That's a beautiful picture you're painting. Will it be for sale?"

Kelly nodded. "Just about everything I paint is for sale. Unless it's something I've made as a gift for someone, that is."

Carolyn glanced around the room, where several framed pictures were on display. "Sometime before I go back to Easton at the end of summer I'd like to buy one of your paintings. It will make a nice gift for our mother's birthday in September."

"If you see something you like now, I'd be happy to hold it for you," Kelly said.

"Hmm . . ." Carolyn tapped her chin. "How about the picture you're working on? I think I'd like that one."

"But it's not done. How can you be sure that's the one you want?"

"I can already see that it's going to be beautiful, so if you'll hold it for me, I'll pick it up before I leave the canal near the end of August."

Elias stood off to one side as the women talked more about Kelly's artwork. It was obvious that Carolyn liked Kelly, and he was sure Carolyn would like Kelly's sister equally well. Elias certainly did.

While Carolyn and Kelly continued to visit, Elias went back to the store and bought a few things they were running low on. He'd just finished shopping when Carolyn joined him at the front counter.

"Think I've got everything you'll need for cooking our meals, but is there anything specific you need or want?" Elias asked her.

She shook her head. "I can't think of anything right now."

"All right then. Let's walk over to the lock tender's house so you can meet Kelly's sister and her children. I'd also like to buy some of Sarah's bread."

Carolyn smiled. "That sounds nice. I've been looking forward to meeting these people you've written me so much about."

When Elias and Carolyn arrived at Sarah's house, Sammy, who'd been walking his dog on the towpath, rushed up to Elias and grabbed hold of his hand. "It's sure good to see ya! Did ya come to take me fishin'?"

"Not today, but maybe this Sunday, if we're back from Mauch Chunk by then."

"I don't think you'll be goin' to Mauch Chunk today," Sammy said with a shake of his head.

"How come?"

"There's a break in the canal, just on the other side of our lock. Mama thinks it was caused by some of the muskrats around here."

"Oh great. That's just one more thing to slow us down. Is the break being fixed?" he asked.

Sammy shrugged. "Beats me."

"Is your mother in the house?"

Sammy nodded. "She's bakin' some bread."

Elias turned to Carolyn. "Let's find out what Sarah knows about the break in the canal."

Sammy led the way, and when they stepped into the house, the delicious aroma of freshly baked bread overwhelmed Elias's senses, causing his mouth to water.

"Mama's in the kitchen, so follow me," Sammy said.

When they entered the kitchen, Sarah turned from the counter where she was working some bread dough and smiled. "It's nice to see you, Elias. Did you come to buy some bread?"

"I did, and I also wanted you to meet my sister." He motioned to Carolyn. "Carolyn's a schoolteacher in Easton, and since she's off for the summer, she decided to join me on the boat for the next few months."

Sarah wiped her floury hands on a dish towel and shook hands with Carolyn. "It's nice to meet you."

Carolyn smiled. "It's delightful to meet you as well. Elias has told me some nice things about you and your family."

Elias's cheeks warmed. He hoped Sarah wouldn't get the wrong idea.

"Well, I can't imagine that he'd have much to tell," Sarah said with a slight nod of her head. "I mean, our life here on the canal isn't all that interesting. It's pretty much the same old thing from day to day."

"You must keep very busy tending the lock," Carolyn said. "That seems like a difficult job to me."

"It's not easy." Sarah glanced toward the door leading to the parlor. "One of the young women from church has been helping me, so that takes some of the inside responsibilities off my shoulders at least."

"I understand that the canal has a break in it right now," Elias said.

Sarah sighed. "I'm afraid so. Some of the men from town are coming down to the canal to fix it today, but you may be stuck here several hours or even overnight before you're able to move on up the canal."

"That's fine with me," Sammy spoke up. "It'll give me a chance to spend time with Elias, and he can finally take me fishin'."

"Maybe Elias has other things to do," Sarah said.

"I'd better offer my help on the canal repairs today, but I'd like to take Sammy and Willis both fishing after church on Sunday afternoon, if that's okay with you," Elias said.

"Well . . ."

"Maybe we could all go," Carolyn spoke up. "We could pack a picnic lunch and make a day of it." She smiled at Sarah. "While Elias and the boys are fishing, you and I can visit and get better acquainted."

"That sounds like fun," Sammy said excitedly. "Can we do that, Mama? Can we, please?"

Elias held his breath as he waited for Sarah's answer and was relieved when she nodded and said, "A picnic lunch does sound like fun. I'll bring some fried chicken, biscuits, some dill pickles, as well as either a cake or some cookies for dessert."

"I'm not much of a baker, but I'd be happy to fix a pot of beans to take along," Carolyn was quick to say.

"And I'll go back over to Mike's store and get several bottles of soda pop for us to drink." Elias thumped Sammy's shoulder. "Why don't you come with me? You can pick out whatever flavors you all like. Maybe we ought to buy a few pieces of candy for you, Willis, and Helen, too."

A wide smile spread across Sammy's face. "Oh boy, I can hardly wait!"

Chapter 21

On Sunday morning, Elias and Carolyn headed to church in Walnutport. The canal repairs had been completed on Saturday evening, and Elias was glad he would be able to resume his trip to Mauch Chunk on Monday morning. He was equally glad for this chance to spend more time in Walnutport. He was looking forward to fishing with Sammy, Willis, and Bobby after church, and also to the picnic lunch they would share with Sarah and her children. He knew this would give Carolyn a chance to get better acquainted with Sarah, and even though he'd never admit it, he was looking forward to spending more time with Sarah, too. She was not only pretty, but kindhearted. She was also a good mother to her children. If it was only possible that she could ever be interested in someone like him.

"You're sure quiet this morning," Carolyn said as they walked side by side. "Is something bothering you?"

He shook his head. "Just thinking is all."

"What are you thinking about?"

"Nothing much. Just thinking about going fishing with Sarah's boys and Bobby."

Carolyn smiled. "You always did like to fish, so I'm sure you'll have a good time. Sammy seemed awfully excited about it yesterday."

"Yes, he did, and I would have taken him fishing right then if I hadn't felt obligated to help the men fix the break in the canal."

"That was important, and I'm sure your help was appreciated."

As they approached the church, Carolyn put her hand in the crook of Elias's arm. "I'm also looking forward to today. Not only going to church, but the picnic with Sarah and her family afterward. Sarah seems so nice, and if we had the chance to spend much time together, I'm sure we could become good friends."

He nodded. "I think you could, too."

When they entered the church, they were greeted by Pastor William, who stood inside the front door.

"Elias, it's good to see you again," the pastor said with a warm smile and a hearty handshake.

"It's good to see you as well." Elias motioned to Carolyn. "This is my sister, Carolyn. She's going to be riding on the boat with me this summer."

Pastor William shook Carolyn's hand. "It's nice to meet you. I'm sure that being on a canal boat will be an interesting experience for you."

She smiled and nodded. "No doubt, and I'm looking forward to enjoying the scenery along the canal when I'm not busy cooking and cleaning for my brother and his helpers."

"Speaking of your helpers," Pastor William

said, looking at Elias, "I take it you didn't have any luck getting Ned or Bobby to come to church with you."

Elias shook his head. "Bobby's so tired after walking the mules all week, he just wants to sleep on Sunday mornings. Sometimes he doesn't wake up until noon. And Ned . . . well, that man is more stubborn than the contrary mule I bought awhile back."

"Maybe he'll decide to join us for one of the services I'll be holding along the canal this summer."

"That would be nice, but I'm not holding my breath."

"God can work a miracle in anyone's life," the pastor said. "I'm just hoping my wife, Betsy, will feel well enough to accompany the singing with her zither during our canal services."

"Is your wife ill?" Carolyn asked.

Pastor William shook his head. "Betsy's expecting a baby, and so far she's had a lot of morning sickness and fatigue."

"That's too bad," Carolyn said. "I hope she'll feel better soon."

"Yes, we're hoping that, too." The pastor motioned to the doors leading to the sanctuary, where the beautiful strains coming from the organ drifted into the foyer. "Betsy's here today, and she'll be playing during our service, but after church is over, she'll need to go home and rest."

"Betsy plays and sings beautifully," Elias told Carolyn.

"You do a pretty fine job of playing that accordion of yours, too." Pastor William thumped Elias on the back. "You should have brought it to the service with you today. You could have either accompanied Betsy or played us a special."

Elias's face heated. "I forgot about bringing it with me, and I'm not sure I'd feel comfortable playing a special by myself."

"Well the next time you're in the area, please bring the accordion and plan to play along with Betsy during our congregational songs."

Elias gave a nod. "Yes, I'll do that."

As Carolyn stood beside Elias, singing the opening hymn in church, her spirits soared. Not only was the song uplifting and lively, but the joy she saw on the people's faces gave her a sense that all was right with the world.

This congregation, made up of many of the townspeople, as well as a few of the canalers and their families, were a friendly bunch who didn't put on airs. The people Carolyn had met before the service had made her feel right at home; not like a stranger visiting their church for the first time.

She glanced at Betsy playing the organ with such enthusiasm. The sincere smile on her face seemed to light up the room.

Carolyn turned her attention to young Sammy Turner. It was so touching when Sammy had entered the sanctuary with his family and plunked down on the pew beside Elias. It was even more touching when Elias smiled and put his arm around the boy's shoulders.

My brother would make a good father, Carolyn thought. *I hope he gets married someday and has a houseful of children.*

Tears pricked the back of her eyes as she thought about her desire to be a wife and mother, but she'd never even had a serious boyfriend. She knew it wasn't because she was unattractive. She'd been told by many people that her shiny blond hair and dazzling blue eyes made her stand out in a crowd. Mother always said Carolyn was holding out for the right man, but the truth was, no man had ever shown her more than a passing interest. It made her wonder if there might be something irritating about her personality that turned men away. Maybe she was too fussy about things, or perhaps she spoke too often when she should have been listening. Whatever the reason, Carolyn had made up her mind that she'd probably spend the rest of her life an old maid schoolteacher, living in a big city with too many people and not enough fresh air.

It was a shame, because she felt relaxed and comfortable here in Walnutport and wished she could live in a small town like this instead of the bustling, ever-growing city of Easton. She knew that wasn't possible, though, because her job was in Easton, and from what Elias had told her, they already had a schoolteacher in Walnutport.

I guess I'll have to enjoy my time on the canal this summer and quit longing for the impossible, she decided. *I just hope I don't disappoint Elias when he finds out that I'm not the world's best cook.*

Soon after church was over, Sarah and her family, along with Elias and Carolyn, headed to a grassy spot near the canal, where they shared the picnic lunch Sarah had made. It was amazing how comfortable she felt with Elias and his sister, and she looked forward to getting to know them both better in the coming weeks.

"Can we go fishin' now?" Sammy asked Elias after he'd finished eating his chicken.

"For goodness' sake, let Elias finish his meal before you start pestering him," Sarah scolded. "We haven't even had our dessert."

"It's all right." Elias wiped his hands on the cloth napkin Sarah had given each of them, and set his plate aside. "We can have our dessert after we've fished awhile."

"Yippee!" Sammy leaped to his feet and grabbed his and Willis's fishing poles. "Let's go find us a good spot to sit and fish!"

Bobby, who had slept all morning on the boat

and then joined them for the picnic, seemed eager to fish, too.

While Elias and the boys headed down the towpath looking for the right spot to fish, Sarah and Carolyn cleared away the dishes, and Helen kept herself entertained by trying to teach Bristle Face to roll over.

"This is such a pleasant way to spend a Sunday afternoon," Carolyn said as she leaned back, resting her elbows on the grass.

Sarah nodded. "Since Sundays are my only day off, I always enjoy every minute. Spending time with family and friends is one of the best ways I know to relax."

"Sunday is Elias's only day off as well. I could see by his expression during lunch that he not only was relaxed, but he also thoroughly enjoyed your fine cooking."

"I'm sure he'll enjoy the cooking you do for him on the boat this summer."

Carolyn shrugged. "The meals I fix might be better than what he's used to having, but they'll pale in comparison to the wonderful fried chicken and biscuits you served us today." She sighed. "My cooking abilities get me by, and I can make most basic meals, but I've never gotten the hang of baking bread or making cakes, cookies, and pies."

"Baking's really not that hard," Sarah said. "It just takes patience and lots of practice. Maybe when you're in the area for a while sometime, you can help me make some of the bread I sell to the boatmen."

Carolyn sucked in her bottom lip. "I'm afraid if the boatmen tasted any baked goods I had made, they'd never buy bread again."

Sarah chuckled. "I'm sure you're not that bad at baking."

"You'd be surprised. Once, when I was still living at home with our folks, I forgot about the cookies I'd put in the oven, and by the time I remembered to check them, they'd turned into little lumps of charcoal. The kitchen was filled with smoke, and the smell of burned cookies lingered for nearly a week. No one in the family wanted me to bake anything after that."

Sarah patted Carolyn's arm. "As I said, I'd be happy to give you a lesson."

"Maybe I'll take you up on that . . . if we're ever in the area long enough, and if you're not too busy with other things."

"Now that Hortence Andrews is coming over every day to help out, I have a little more time for baking and other things when I'm not letting boats through the canal. So I'm sure I could find the time."

Carolyn pointed to where Elias and the boys sat on some boulders near the canal, a little distance away. "I think my brother's having just as much fun fishing as your two boys are."

Sarah shielded her eyes from the glare of the sun as she studied Elias holding his fishing pole with one hand, while his other hand rested on Sammy's shoulder.

Sarah smiled. It was good for her boys to enjoy the company of a man. Since Sam died, they didn't get to do many fun things, and Sammy had taken such a liking to Elias, looking up to him almost like he was his father.

Elias seems like such a nice man. If only he wasn't a boatman, Sarah thought with regret.

Chapter 22

*A*s Patrick walked along the dusty towpath in the direction of Sarah's house, he kicked at every stone in his way. He'd heard that Sarah and her children had gone on a picnic with Elias and his sister on Sunday afternoon, and that worried him. He'd also heard from one of the boatmen who'd seen them on Sunday that Elias had taken a special interest in Sarah's son Sammy and taken him fishing. Patrick was even more convinced that Elias was using the boy to get close to Sarah.

"I can't let that happen," Patrick mumbled. "I lost Sarah to Sam Turner when we were teenagers, and I'm not gonna lose her to some canaler who has nothing to offer but fancy words and a dingy boat full of dirty coal."

By the time Patrick got to Sarah's house, he was

so worked up that he had to stop and take in a few deep breaths. It wouldn't be good to let his Irish temper take over. He had more self-control than that. He'd convinced himself that the best thing he could do was try to win Sarah's heart by being nice and offering to help her with anything she needed.

Patrick was about to knock on Sarah's front door, when it swung open suddenly and that shaggy terrier of hers leaped out at him, barking and showing its teeth.

"Come back here, Bristle Face!" Sammy shouted as he grabbed the dog's collar. "And quit that yappety-yapping!"

The dog's barking changed to a low growl, as though he was warning Patrick not to come any closer.

Patrick cleared his throat a couple of times. "Uh . . . is your mama in the house?"

Sammy gave a nod. "She and Hortence are fixin' some sandwiches for our lunch."

At the mention of food, Patrick's stomach growled. He'd shoed several horses this morning and had only taken time for a quick cup of coffee and a stale piece of bread. Maybe if he played it right, Sarah would invite him to join them for lunch.

"I suppose ya wanna come in," Sammy said, crinkling his freckled nose as he squinted up at Patrick.

"Yes, I sure would."

"Well, go on in the kitchen then. I'm takin' Bristle Face out for a walk, but I'll be back in time for lunch." The boy hurried away, and Patrick stepped into the house.

He found Sarah and Hortence in the kitchen, with their backs toward him as they worked at the counter. Willis and Helen sat at the table, staring at Sarah's back with anxious expressions. He thought they looked like a couple of baby birds waiting to be fed.

"Oh my, you startled me, Patrick!" Sarah said when Patrick cleared his throat to announce his presence. "I didn't hear you knock on the door."

"I didn't knock. I ran into Sammy when he was coming out the door to take his dog for a walk, and he said you were in here and that I should come in."

"Oh, I see. Well, what can I do for you? Are you in need of more bread?"

He gave a nod. "I just have a few pieces left, and what I do have has gotten stale."

"I only have a few loaves right now," Sarah said, "but I can sell you one of those if you think that'll be enough."

"One should do me fine." Patrick glanced at the pieces of bread Sarah had been buttering. "What kind of sandwiches are you making?"

"Some will be just jelly for the kids," Hortence spoke up before Sarah could respond. She smiled at Patrick. "And we'll make a few sandwiches with leftover chicken."

Patrick's stomach rumbled and he licked his lips. "Umm . . . I haven't had a chicken sandwich in a long time."

"If you haven't had lunch yet, you're welcome to join us," Sarah said.

Patrick nodded eagerly. "I haven't eaten anything since early this morning, so I appreciate the invite."

Sarah motioned to the table. "Take a seat. We'll have these sandwiches made in no time, and then we can eat."

Patrick pulled out a chair and took a seat beside Willis. "I heard you went fishing the other day," he said, hoping to win the boy over.

Willis bobbed his head. "Didn't catch nothin', but we sure had fun. Elias told me and Sammy lots of funny stories 'bout when he was boy."

"I have some funny stories to tell from my childhood. Would you like to hear one of 'em?" Patrick asked.

Willis shrugged. "I guess so."

"Well, once when I was helpin' my pa shoe an ornery mule, the crazy critter grabbed hold of Pop's shirtsleeve and bit a hole right through it."

Willis frowned. "Don't see what's so funny 'bout that. If a mule woulda made a hole in my shirt, I'da been real mad."

"My pa did get mad, but it was funny to see that

old mule holding a piece of Pop's shirt between its teeth while she shook her head from side to side."

"I'll bet that did look pretty funny," Hortence spoke up as she placed a platter of sandwiches on the table. "If I'd been there, I'm sure I would have laughed." She gave Patrick a wide smile and plunked down in the chair on the other side of him. "I think we're ready to eat. We just need to wait for Sammy to get back from walking the dog."

"Here he is now," Sarah said as Sammy stepped into the room. "Go to the sink and wash your hands, son."

"Okay, Mama." Sammy cast Patrick a quick glance, then ambled across the room to the sink, where, using both hands, he pulled the handle of the pump several times for some fresh water. When he returned and took a seat across from Patrick, Sarah set a pitcher of milk on the table, and then she seated herself next to Helen.

"Close your eyes, kids; I'm going to pray," Sarah said sweetly.

Patrick, not being the religious type, never prayed when he ate a meal, but out of respect for Sarah, he bowed his head.

"Dear Lord," she prayed in a sincere tone, "we thank You for this food we're about to eat. Bless it, and use it to strengthen our bodies. Amen."

Everyone dug in, and Patrick savored his first bite of the chicken sandwich. How nice it would be to have a wife waiting for him at home each evening with a tasty meal on the table.

He leaned closer to Sarah. "Say, I was wondering if you'd like to—"

Wo–o–o–o! Wo–o–o–o! The moaning of a conch shell floated through the kitchen window.

"I'd better go get ready for that boat," Sarah said, pushing her chair away from the table.

Patrick jumped up. "Would you like me to help you open the lock?"

She shook her head. "Thanks anyway, but I can manage. Just have a seat and enjoy your lunch. I'll be back soon."

Sarah hurried out the door so quickly that Patrick couldn't even formulate a response. He sat back down and took another bite of his sandwich.

"Do you like it?" Hortence asked. "Is there enough butter on your bread?"

"It's just fine. Very tasty, in fact."

She smiled at him. "Maybe you'd like to come over to my house for supper sometime. Mother likes it when we have guests."

A trickle of sweat ran down Patrick's forehead. Was Hortence making a play for him? The look he saw on her face did appear kind of desperate, and the fact that she was nearly thirty years old and still not married made him wonder if she might be looking for a husband. Well, if she had him in mind, she could forget it. The only woman he wanted was Sarah.

• • •

After Elias had picked up a load of coal at Mauch Chunk on Monday afternoon, he'd been surprised at the way Wilma, their stubborn mule, had cooperated with Bobby. Not only was she walking faster, but she was no longer picking on Dolly. Maybe she'd finally come to know her place and had decided to cooperate. Maybe things would go better for them now, and they wouldn't lose so much time.

"Are you planning to stop in Walnutport today?" Carolyn asked as she joined Elias at the bow of the boat.

He shook his head. "Thanks to that break in the canal and several days of dealing with a contrary mule, I've already lost too much time. So I think it's best if we keep heading straight for Easton."

"I suppose you're right." Carolyn sighed. "I enjoyed being with Sarah so much the other day and was hoping I might have the chance to visit with her again."

"I'm sure there will other times for visiting," Elias said. "I plan to stop in Walnutport whenever I can for church, and since Sarah doesn't work on Sundays, she'll have more time to visit then, anyway."

"I don't know how Sarah manages her job. It seems like such hard work."

Elias nodded. "I don't think it's the kind of work

a woman should do, but Sarah seems to manage okay."

"Mind if I ask you a personal question?"

"What's that?"

"I was wondering if you might be interested in Sarah."

His eyebrows shot up. "What would make you think that?"

"I couldn't help but notice the smile on your face when we were with Sarah and her children on Sunday. You seemed very content."

"I did enjoy being with them, but Sarah's just a friend and will never be anything more."

"How do you know?"

"Because I'm sure that a pretty woman like her would never be interested in someone like me."

"What's that supposed to mean?"

He touched the side of his face. "Who would want a man with an ugly birthmark?"

"You're too sensitive about that." Carolyn placed her hand on his arm. "Mother's told you this before, and I'm going to say it again now. When the right woman comes along, she won't even notice that red mark on your face. What really counts is what's in a person's heart, not his outward appearance."

Elias shrugged. "I wish that were true, but I grew up hearing the jeers and taunts from others about my ugly red mark, and no woman has ever shown me more than a passing interest. I've come to accept the fact that true love will probably never happen for me."

"That's ridiculous. If you'd just relax and let your charming and sensitive personality shine through, you could win any woman's heart."

"Ya can't be charmin' or sensitive and be a boatman," Ned said, stepping up to them. "A boatman's gotta be tough as nails."

"Like you?" Elias asked with a grin.

Ned lifted his bearded chin. "Yep, just like me."

Elias rolled his eyes, and Carolyn snickered quietly. Then she tapped Elias on the shoulder and said, "I'm going below to make some soup for lunch. Should I bring you up a cup when it's ready?"

"That'd be fine. Ned can take over steering the boat while I eat lunch, and then I'll take over leading the mules so Bobby can come aboard and eat."

"Okay." Carolyn turned and hurried away.

Ned looked at Elias and frowned. "When do I get to eat?"

"You can either eat before I do, or wait until Bobby is done."

"Guess I'll go first. I work better when my belly's full."

"I would have suggested that we tie the boat up for a while and all eat together," Elias said, "but we've lost enough time these last few weeks."

"That's for sure." Ned leaned over the boat and

spit a wad of chewing tobacco into the canal. "You never shoulda bought that stupid mule from the blacksmith in Walnutport."

"If you'll recall, there were no other mules available," Elias reminded. "And as I'm sure you must have noticed, Wilma seems to be behaving herself much better now."

"Yeah, I guess." Ned spat another hunk of tobacco into the water. "At least for now, she is."

"I think she just needed to get used to walking with Dolly and learn what she's supposed to do."

Ned opened his mouth like he was about to respond, when a bloodcurdling scream from below caused them both to jump. Elias turned the tiller over to Ned and raced down the stairs.

Chapter 23

"*W*hat's wrong?" Elias called as he rushed into the galley.

Carolyn turned from the stove and held up her left hand. "I burned myself on the stove," she said tearfully. "It hurts so bad I can barely stand the pain."

Elias stepped closer and examined her hand. Several ugly blisters had already formed, and all of her fingers looked red and swollen. "We'd better stop in Walnutport, after all," he said. "I think you need to be seen by a doctor. In the meantime, you'd better take a seat at the table and put your hand in some cold water to help with the pain."

"I'm so sorry about this." Carolyn's chin trembled and her eyes filled with tears.

Elias shook his head. "You have nothing to be sorry for. It was an accident, plain and simple."

"But if you stop in Walnutport so I can see the doctor, you'll be losing more time, which is exactly what you didn't want to do."

"Your needs come before my schedule, so stop worrying about it and take a seat at the table."

She sighed deeply and did as he asked. When he set a pan of cold water in front of her, she plunged her hand in and gasped. "It still hurts, Elias. It hurts so much!"

"I'm sure it does, but you'd better keep it there until we reach Walnutport."

Elias turned and hurried back to the main deck. He knew it was important for Carolyn to see the doctor, and right now it didn't matter how long it took to make his coal delivery.

By the time Sarah got around to eating her lunch, the children had finished and gone over to Mike and Kelly's to play with their cousins. When she stepped into the kitchen, she was surprised to see that Patrick was still there, sitting at the table with Hortence and drinking coffee.

"I didn't realize you were still here," Sarah said to Patrick. "I figured by now you'd be back working in your blacksmith shop."

He shook his head. "I was waiting for you. I wanted to ask if you—"

Wo–o–o–o! Wo–o–o–o! "It sounds like another boat's coming through." Sarah groaned. "At this rate, I'll never get to eat my sandwich."

"I wish you'd let me help you outside," Patrick said. "We could get the job done twice as fast with the two of us working."

Sarah flapped her hand. "Tending the lock is my responsibility, and it really doesn't take that long. The problem today has been that too many boats have come through in such a short time." She started for the door, but turned back. "Please don't let me keep you from whatever work you might have in your shop."

"Guess you're right. I really oughta get back. I'll be by to see you again in a few days." He stood and moved toward the door, and she hurried out behind him.

Just as Sarah approached the lockgate, she spotted Elias's boat, which was almost at the lock. "I have a few loaves of bread left if you want any today," she called.

He shook his head. "Not this time, but we do need to stop. Carolyn burned her hand real bad, and she needs to see the doctor."

"Oh no! I'm sorry to hear that."

When Elias's boat had gone through the lock, she pointed to a post on the other side of it. "You can tie up here, if you like."

"Thanks."

Elias had no more than docked his boat when another boat came through. As much as Sarah wanted to see how badly Carolyn had been burned, she knew she had a job to do.

"When you get done at the doctor's, stop by and let me know how Carolyn's doing," she called to Elias.

"All right, we will."

Sarah whispered a prayer on behalf of Elias's sister and hurried to do her job.

"I really don't think it's necessary for me to stay here in Walnutport," Carolyn said as she and Elias left the doctor's office later. "I can stay on the boat with you and change my own bandage every day."

Elias shook his head. "That's not a good idea. What if infection sets in? If you don't want to stay in Walnutport, then when we get to Easton, I should drop you off at Mother and Father's."

"No way! Father didn't want me to join you on the boat, so if he knew about my hand, he'd give me a hard time and probably blame you for it, saying that the conditions on your boat are crude and unsafe." She cringed at the remembrance of her father's earlier words. "And Mother would hover around me all day and treat me as if I'm a little girl. I think the best thing we can do is go over to the boardinghouse Dr. McGrath recommended and see if they have room for me to stay there."

"I suppose we could do that, but I think I might have a better idea."

"What's that?"

"We could see if Sarah would be willing to let you stay at her place. I heard that Sarah's mother-in-law used to live with her, so I'm sure she has the room."

"I don't know if that's such a good idea. Sarah has enough on her hands, tending the lock and taking care of her three children. She doesn't need me to look after."

"I'm not suggesting that she look after you, because I'm sure you can manage to look after yourself," Elias said. "What I was thinking was that I'd be willing to pay Sarah for your room and board, and since I'm sure she could use the extra money . . ."

"Ah, I see now. You're concerned about Sarah and are looking for some way to help her out."

His face turned red as he slowly nodded. "She has a lot of responsibility on her shoulders. I also know that she doesn't make a lot of money tending the lock, and I'm sure that selling bread to the boatmen doesn't bring in much either."

"I understand your concerns, but what if Sarah would rather not have a near-stranger staying with her?"

Elias shrugged. "Well, we won't know until we

ask, and if she says no, then you can rest on the boat while I head over to the boardinghouse and see about getting you a room."

Carolyn contemplated the idea and finally nodded. If she had her preference, it would be to stay with Sarah.

Chapter 24

"*I* can't thank you enough for letting me stay here with you," Carolyn told Sarah several days later as they cleared the dishes from the breakfast table. She lifted her left hand, still wrapped in a gauze bandage. "The salve and herbs Dr. McGrath gave me for the burn are working quite well, and I've enjoyed being here with you and the children."

Sarah smiled as she pushed a wayward strand of hair away from her face. "We've enjoyed having you here and will miss you when you join Elias again."

Carolyn set the dirty plates in the sink. "I hope things are going okay for him. From all that he's told me, it seems as if he's had nothing but trouble since he took over our grandfather's boat. If Father knew about everything that had gone wrong, he'd say to Elias, 'I told you so, son.'"

"A lot of things can go wrong for the boatmen, as well as those who live and work along the canal." Sarah slowly shook her head. "I can't begin to tell you about all the accidents that have occurred over the past few years, just along the stretch of canal that runs by Walnutport."

"I understand that your husband was killed in an accident involving the canal."

Sarah blinked against unwanted tears. She always felt weepy when she thought about Sam's untimely death. "He was crushed between a boat and the lock," she murmured. "I'm just grateful Sam found the Lord before he died, because I have the assurance that he's in heaven now and someday we'll be reunited."

"As Christians, we do have that consolation," Carolyn agreed. "It makes me wonder how those who haven't had a personal relationship with Christ deal with death and other tragedies that occur in their lives."

Sarah stared out the window, watching a pair of geese floating on the canal. "Several of the boatmen have come to know the Lord after attending one of the services Pastor William holds along the canal, but there are many others who are still deeply rooted in their sinful way of life."

Carolyn nodded. "I think Elias's helper is one of those. From what I've seen, Ned has several nasty habits, and he sometimes uses foul language and even takes the Lord's name in vain. It makes me wonder why Elias puts up with him and his crude ways."

"I understand that Ned used to work for your

grandfather, so maybe Elias feels a sense of responsibility toward Ned."

"I believe you're right about that. I also think Elias believes that in time Ned will see his need to change and give his heart to the Lord."

"With Elias setting the example of Christianity, maybe Ned will become a Christian someday." Sarah took a sack of flour down from the cupboard. "Would you like me to teach you my secret for making light and airy bread?"

"Yes, I would. I'd like to learn how to make the dough dab bread you fixed to go with the stew we had for supper last night, too."

Sarah slipped her apron over her head. "I'd be happy to teach you to make dough dab. Hopefully, the boats coming through the lock today will be far enough apart that we'll have time to get lots of baking done."

"With your baking skills, I'm wondering . . . Have you ever considered opening a bakery?"

"The idea has crossed my mind," Sarah replied, "but I'm sure the rent on a building in town would be expensive, so I doubt that I'd ever be able to afford it."

"Well, it's always nice to have a goal and something to plan for."

"Yes, and if I owned my own bakery I could give up lock tending."

The sound of giggling coming from the parlor could be heard, and Sarah smiled. "Since

Hortence has been coming to help out, she keeps my kids well entertained, which helps me get more done. Before, even when Maria was here to help, the kids always seemed to be competing for my attention."

"It's good that she's such a big help with the children."

A knock sounded on the door, interrupting their conversation. "I'll get that!" Hortence called from the other room over Bristle Face's frantic barking.

A few seconds later, she entered the kitchen with Patrick at her side and Bristle Face nipping at his heels.

"Stop it, Bristle Face," Sarah scolded. "Sammy, come get your dog!"

Sammy rushed into the room and swept Bristle Face into his arms. "Sorry, Mama. He got away from me when Hortence went to answer the door."

"Just make sure you keep that stupid mutt away from me," Patrick said roughly. "I'm gettin' sick of him yappin' and snappin' every time I come around."

Sammy's eyes narrowed. "Bristle Face ain't stupid, and he only barks at people he don't like."

Sarah frowned. "That'll be enough, Sammy. Just take the dog outside for a walk."

"He was outside awhile ago, so I don't think he's gotta go again."

Sarah pointed to the door. "Just do as I said."

Sammy ambled out the door mumbling under his breath.

Sarah turned to Patrick and smiled. "Sorry about that. I don't know why Bristle Face is so testy around you."

"You heard what the boy said. The dog doesn't like me, though I can't figure out why. I've never done nothin' to make him mad."

"Some dogs are temperamental," Carolyn spoke up. "They pick out certain people to bark at for no particular reason."

Patrick swung his gaze from Sarah to Carolyn. "Don't think I've met you before. Are you new to the area?"

Sarah introduced Carolyn to Patrick and explained that she was Elias's sister. Then she told Carolyn that Patrick was the town's blacksmith.

Carolyn smiled and explained why she was staying with Sarah.

"It's nice of Sarah to take you in." He glanced back at Sarah and grinned. " 'Course she's always been kind to others."

Sarah felt the heat of a blush creep up her neck and cascade over her cheeks. "It's a Christian's duty to help others, and with Carolyn staying here, the two of us have become good friends."

Carolyn nodded. "Sarah's going to teach me the secret of making good bread."

Patrick smacked his lips. "Well, you've got a

good teacher, 'cause nobody bakes bread any tastier than Sarah's."

Sarah's cheeks grew hotter. "I don't think my bread's anything special."

"You're wrong about that; your bread's the best I've ever had." Patrick took a step closer to Sarah. "I was wonderin' if I could talk to you alone for a few minutes."

"I guess so." Sarah motioned to the door. "Should we go outside?"

"Sure, that'd be fine."

"I'll be right back," Sarah said to Carolyn. "You can fix yourself a cup of tea while I'm gone if you like."

"I might just do that." Carolyn smiled at Patrick. "It was nice meeting you."

"Same here," Patrick said as he went out the door.

Sarah stepped out behind him. "What was it you wanted to talk to me about?"

Patrick cleared his throat a few times and glanced around as though he was afraid someone might hear their conversation, which Sarah thought was silly. Sammy was way down the towpath with Bristle Face, and no one else was around.

"I . . . uh . . . was wondering if you'd go on a picnic with me this Sunday," he said in a near whisper.

Sarah shook her head. "I've told you before, Patrick. We always go to church on Sundays."

"I know that," he said with an exasperated groan. "I was talkin' about after church."

"I won't be free in the afternoon because Pastor William will be holding another preaching service along the canal after the service in town. He plans to baptize several people in the canal."

"Are you gettin' baptized, Sarah?"

"No, I've already been baptized."

"Then there's no need for you to go."

"Yes, there is. I know several of the folks who are getting baptized, so I want to attend the service to offer my support and approval."

"I see." Patrick pursed his lips as he tapped his foot. "It makes it kinda hard for us to court when you have to be here to let boats through the lock six days a week, and then on Sundays you always seem to have other plans."

Sarah's mouth fell open. "You—you think we're courting?"

He shrugged. "I guess not officially, but I'd like for us to be. Fact is, I've cared for you ever since we were kids, and—"

She held up her hand. "You're a nice man, Patrick, but I really can't think about being courted by anyone right now."

"How come?"

"I have a job to do, three kids to raise, and as you mentioned, very little free time."

"Then why don't we skip the courtin' part and just get married?"

173

"Wh–what?"

"I said why don't we—"

"I heard what you said. I'm just shocked that you said it."

"But I've been interested in you since we were kids. Fact is, if you hadn't run off with Sam when you did, I'd planned to court you."

Sarah leaned against the porch railing, feeling the need for some support. She'd had no idea Patrick felt that way about her when they were children. Although in the last few months, she'd suspected he was interested in her now. But the thought of marrying him hadn't even entered her mind.

Wo–o–o–o! Wo–o–o–o! The sound of a conch shell pulled Sarah's thoughts aside. "A boat's coming. I'll need to get the lock opened, so I'm afraid I can't talk any longer."

She started to move away, but he reached out and touched her arm. "Would you at least think about what I said and let me know when you have an answer?"

She gave a brief nod and hurried off to open the lock.

"Sure am glad we're not far from Walnutport," Ned said, joining Elias at the bow of the boat. "I'm out of chewin' tobacco again and need to stop at the store."

Elias shook his head slowly as he rolled his

eyes. He wished Ned would give up that nasty habit, but he'd been doing it for a good many years, so it wasn't likely he'd give it up now. Some things, no matter how much he wanted them, just weren't meant to be.

"Does that shake of your head mean we're not stoppin' at Walnutport?" Ned asked, bumping Elias's arm.

"Of course we're stopping. I want to check on Carolyn. I was shaking my head because I can't understand why you think you need that awful chewing tobacco."

Ned merely shrugged in reply; then he leaned over the boat and hollered at Bobby, "Get them mules movin' faster! When they start laggin' like that, you need to take control!"

Bobby swatted Wilma's rump, and the next thing Elias knew the crazy mule let out a loud bray and kicked her left foot back. Bobby screamed and crumpled to the ground.

Chapter 25

"*M*y leg hurts!" Bobby wailed. "I've never had anything hurt so much!"

As soon as Elias looked at Bobby's twisted leg he knew it was broken. White-hot anger boiled in his chest. That stupid mule the blacksmith sold him had caused nothing but trouble, and now his young mule driver had been put out of commission because of the stubborn, temperamental critter.

"I'm real sorry," Bobby said, tears streaming down his face. "I shoulda never slapped that ornery mule on the rump."

Elias scooped the boy into his arms and carried him onto the boat. "It wasn't your fault. You were only doing what Ned told you to do."

"I know, but I shoulda realized Wilma was still fidgety and might decide to pull somethin' on me."

"It's okay." Elias carried Bobby down to his cabin and laid him carefully on the bunk. "We're almost to Walnutport, and as soon as we arrive we'll take you to see Dr. McGrath."

"B–but who's gonna lead the mules?"

"I will, and Ned can steer the boat."

Elias splinted the boy's leg with two pieces of wood and then tied a strip of cloth around it. "Now just lie here and try to relax. We'll be in Walnutport soon."

The first thing Elias did when they arrived in Walnutport was to take Bobby to see Dr. McGrath. While the doctor took care of Bobby's leg, Elias went to tell Bobby's aunt Martha what had happened. After he returned to the doctor's office and picked up Bobby, he took him to the boardinghouse so his aunt could care for him, then he returned to the boat where he'd left Ned.

"How's the kid?" Ned asked. "Did ya get him to the doctor okay?"

Elias nodded. "His leg's broken pretty bad, and he'll have to be off it for a good many weeks."

"Figured as much." Ned grunted. "Now you'll need to find another mule driver somewhere."

"You're right, and another mule, too." Elias frowned. "I've had it with that animal! In fact, I'm taking her right back to the blacksmith!"

Ned's forehead wrinkled. "What if Patrick don't want the critter back?"

Elias shrugged. "I won't know until I go over there and ask. Are you coming or staying?"

"Think I'll come along. If Patrick gives you a problem about the mule, I wouldn't wanna miss out on a fight between you two."

Elias shook his head. "There won't be any fighting. I'm just going to take the mule back and ask Patrick to refund my money."

Ned let out a low whistle. "This I've gotta see."

Patrick had just finished repairing the wheel on a wagon owned by one of the farmers in the area, when Elias showed up. His helper, Ned, was with him, leading the mule Patrick had sold Elias several weeks ago.

"What can I do for you?" Patrick asked.

"I'm here to return your mule."

Patrick shook his head. "She ain't my mule. You paid for the critter, fair and square, so she's your mule now."

"She's not working out for me," Elias said.

"She's been nothing but trouble since the day I got her."

"That's not my problem. Maybe you just need to work harder with her . . . get her trained."

"We've been working with her, and as far as I'm concerned, she's not trainable. The stupid animal kicked my mule driver this morning and broke his leg."

Patrick ground his teeth together. "If I'd have known the fool mule would do somethin' like that, I'd never have sold her to you."

"Then you'll take her back?"

Patrick shook his head. "Don't know what I'd do with her if I did."

"You could sell her to someone else," Ned spoke up. "Someone who has the time and patience to work with her."

Patrick contemplated things a few seconds then finally nodded. "Tell ya what I'll do. I'll take the mule and give you back half your money."

Elias's eyebrows furrowed. "Why only half?"

"You've used her awhile, so she's worth less to me now."

A muscle on the side of Elias's neck quivered. "That's not fair. The mule's worth what I paid, and—"

"Take it or leave it."

"We'll take it," Ned cut in. He handed the mule's rope to Patrick. "Any idea where we can find another mule?"

Patrick scratched the side of his head. "Let's see now. I believe Slim Collier has a couple of mules he uses on his farm, but I doubt he'd be willing to part with either of 'em."

Elias frowned. "Do you know of any other mules I might buy?"

"I think maybe Gus over at the livery stable has one now."

"Guess I'll head over to his place and see." Elias hesitated a minute and then held out his hand. "What about the money you owe me for returning your mule?"

Patrick reached into his pants pocket and pulled out twenty-five dollars. It irked him that he had to take the mule back, but he didn't want the fancy boatman going around town blabbing to everyone that Patrick O'Grady was unfair in his business dealings. So he'd take the dumb mule and hopefully make a profit when he found someone else willing to buy the critter.

"Isn't that Elias's boat tied up over there by Mike and Kelly's store?" Sarah asked Carolyn as the two women hung clean clothes on the line.

Carolyn shielded her eyes from the glare of the sun. "I believe it is. I don't see any sign of Elias or his helpers, though."

"Maybe they're in the store. If you'd like to walk over there and see, I'll finish hanging the last of these towels."

"I'll wait until we're done," Carolyn said. "That way if a boat comes through and you need to open the lock, I'll be able to finish hanging the laundry for you."

Sarah smiled. Carolyn was such a thoughtful person. "I appreciate your help, and I'm going to miss you when you join Elias on his boat again."

Carolyn smiled, too. "I'll miss you as well. These last two weeks have been fun, even though I was in a lot of pain the first few days." She glanced at her hand, almost completely healed from the burns.

"They've been fun for me, too. Between you and Hortence, I've had more help than I know what to do with."

Carolyn chuckled. "I can't believe you said that. No one as busy as you can ever have too much help."

"I guess that's true." Sarah glanced at the towpath and saw Elias heading their way, while Ned, leading a mule, turned in the direction of Elias's boat. "Here comes your brother now," she said, pointing in that direction.

Carolyn squinted. "I don't see Bobby though, and I wonder if Ned's leading the mule because they took it to the blacksmith to have it shod."

Sarah shrugged. "I don't know, but that looks like a different mule to me."

A few minutes later, Elias joined them under the clothesline. "Hello, ladies."

"Hello, Elias," Sarah said.

"It's good to see you." Carolyn stepped forward and gave him a hug.

"It's good to see you, too. How's your hand?"

"Much better. Dr. McGrath said as long as I keep it clean and continue to put the ointment on, I should be fine."

"That's good to hear, because I really need you on the boat again."

"How come? Hasn't Ned been feeding you well enough?"

"We've managed okay until this morning."

"What happened?" Sarah asked.

"That troublesome mule I bought from the blacksmith kicked Bobby and broke his leg." Elias groaned. "I returned the mule to Patrick and got half my money back; then I bought another mule from the man who runs the livery stable. This creature seems to have a more agreeable temperament, so hopefully she'll work out better than the last one. My big concern is that I have no one to lead the mules." He scuffed the toe of his boot and looked at Sarah. "I don't suppose you'd consider letting Sammy come to work for me until he goes back to school at the end of summer?"

Her spine stiffened, and she glared at him. "How can you even ask me that? After my reaction when Sammy ran off to lead your mules before, you ought to know how I feel about it."

"I understand your concerns, but I'll take good care of him and make sure—"

"Absolutely not! None of my kids will ever work on this canal!" Sarah turned and tromped into the house.

Chapter 26

*A*s Elias's boat headed toward Mauch Chunk, with Ned steering and Elias leading the mules, he fumed with every step he took. He didn't like having to lead the mules when he should have been on the boat. Well, at least the new mule he'd bought was more cooperative than the last one, and since Elias had no one else to lead the mules, he had no choice but to take over that responsibility. If he could only have had Sammy working for him, it would have helped a lot, but that wasn't to be.

Elias knew he'd upset Sarah by asking if Sammy could work for him and wished he hadn't brought it up. He figured he'd ruined whatever chances he may have had with Sarah—if he'd ever had any chance at all. He'd seen the way she couldn't make eye contact with him most of the time. She probably couldn't stand to look at the ugly red mark on his face.

As they drew closer to Mauch Chunk, Elias spotted a young, red-haired boy running after a chicken along the edge of the towpath.

"What are you doing with that chicken?" Elias called.

The boy screeched to a halt and turned to face Elias, his eyes wide with fear. "I . . . uh . . ."

"Is it your chicken?"

"No, sir. I was tryin' to catch it so my ma would have somethin' to fix us for supper tonight. Somethin' besides beans."

Elias studied the boy a few seconds. He was barefooted, wore a pair of tattered trousers and a faded blue shirt, and looked to be about ten years old.

"What's your name and where do you live?" Elias asked.

The boy stared at the ground and dragged his big toe through the dirt. "My name's Frank. Me and my two sisters live in a shack with our ma."

"Near Mauch Chunk?"

"Yeah."

"What about your father? Is he a canaler?"

Frank shook his head. "Pa used to work at the coal mines in Mauch Chunk, but now he's dead. Ma washes clothes for the boatmen sometimes, but she don't make much and can't hardly feed us no more."

Elias's heart clenched. There were so many poor people living along the canal. He wished he could help them all.

"How would you like to come to work for me?"

"Doin' what?"

Elias motioned to his mules. "Leading them while they pull my boat."

Frank's pale eyebrows shot up. "Really?"

"That's right. The mule driver I had has a broken leg, so I need someone to take over the job for the rest of the summer."

"I'd like to earn some money to help my ma, but I've never led a mule before."

"I'll teach you."

"That'd be great." Frank nodded enthusiastically. "I'll have to run home and tell Ma first, though."

"I'll tell you what," Elias said. "I'll get my load of coal in Mauch Chunk and meet up with you here in a couple of hours."

Frank offered Elias a toothless grin. "Sounds good to me."

Elias reached into his pants pocket and pulled out a five dollar bill. "Give this to your mother, so she can buy something to eat. And no more stealing chickens," he added as he handed the money to Frank.

"Wow! Thanks, mister."

"My name's Elias Brooks, but you can just call me Elias."

"Okay. See you soon, Elias!" Frank waved and hurried away.

Elias hoped he hadn't made a mistake. For all he knew, Frank might not even be the boy's real name. For that matter, he might never see the boy again. Well, if that was the case, then so be it.

Elias had done what he felt was right, and he'd just wait and see if Frank was waiting for him when he came back.

As Patrick headed for Cooper's store, he struggled with the urge to stop over at the lock tender's house and talk to Sarah. After he'd blurted out the way he felt about her the other day and suggested that they get married, he wasn't sure if he should give her some time to think about things or keep trying to pursue her. One thing he knew was that he'd never get anywhere with Sarah if he couldn't spend more time with her so he could show her what a good husband he'd make. Since Sunday was her only day off and she spent part of it in church, he'd come to the conclusion that he needed to attend church, too. Maybe Sarah wouldn't mind if he sat beside her during the service.

Of course, he reasoned, *that will mean sitting beside those kids of hers, and one in particular doesn't like me very much.*

Patrick leaned over, picked up a flat rock, and tossed it into the canal, the way he'd done many times when he was a boy. There had to be some way for him to win Sammy over.

When he entered the store a few minutes later, his gaze came to rest on the glass-topped counter full of candy. Ah, that might be just what he needed!

185

He studied the variety of candy—gumdrops, lemon drops, horehound drops, licorice ropes, peppermint sticks, and several kinds of lollipops. *Hmm . . . which one should I choose?*

"Can I help you with something?" Mike asked, positioning himself on the other side of the counter.

"I'm lookin' to buy some candy, but I'm not sure what kind. Have you got any suggestions?"

"Guess that all depends on what kind you like."

Patrick shook his head. "It ain't for me. It's for Sarah's kids, but I was hopin' to get the kind that Sammy likes best."

"Oh, that's easy then. I know exactly what my nephew likes." Mike picked up the jar of lollipops. "Sammy likes cherry—although he'll eat most any kind except orange. His little sister likes orange, though. I think Willis does, too."

"All right then, I'll take two orange lollipops and one cherry." Patrick smiled. He could hardly wait to see the kids' expressions when he gave them the candy on Sunday after church.

As Elias led the mules down the towpath coming out of Mauch Chunk, he looked for Frank, but saw no sign of the boy. *He's probably not coming,* Elias told himself. *Either his mother said no, or he took off with the money I gave him and never said a word to his mother about working for me.* He flicked at a fly that kept buzzing his head. *Guess that's what I get for being so nice, but I couldn't help feeling sorry for the boy.*

"Hey, mister—I mean, Elias. I've been watchin' for you!"

When Frank stepped out of the bushes, Elias jumped, causing both mules to bray and nearly run into his back.

"Sorry. Didn't mean to scare ya." Frank looked up at Elias and squinted his blue eyes. "If ya haven't changed your mind about me leadin' your mules, I'm ready to go." He lifted the small satchel he held in his hands. "Don't have many clothes, but Ma said I'd need another pair of trousers to wear, and I've also got an old pair of my pa's boots, 'cause she said I might need 'em if my feet get too sore from walkin' the towpath."

"Does that mean your mother's okay with you working for me the rest of this summer?"

"Yeah, sure. Said I could work clear up to the time the canal closes for the winter."

"What about school? Won't you need to quit so you can return to school in the fall?"

Frank shook his head. "Don't need no schoolin'. Pa didn't have much, and he got by."

Elias was tempted to argue with the boy but figured he'd wait until summer was nearing an end and then bring up the subject again.

"So what should I do to make the mules go?" Frank asked.

"If you walk along with me for a while, I'll

teach you all you need to know about leading the mules." Elias gave the boy's shoulder a gentle squeeze.

"What are their names?"

"The lead mule is Dolly. She's been with me since the beginning of the season. I just got the other mule and haven't named her yet, so if you have any ideas, I'm open to suggestions."

"How 'bout Jenny?"

Elias considered that a few seconds and finally nodded. "Jenny sounds like a good name to me."

They walked together for a time; then Elias handed the lead rope to Frank, staying close to the boy to be sure both mules cooperated.

When they reached Walnutport sometime later, Carolyn leaned over the edge of the boat and called to Elias, "Can we spend the night in Walnutport and go to church tomorrow morning?"

"I don't think so," he shouted in return.

"Why not?"

"I just hadn't planned on stopping, that's all." Elias wasn't about to tell Carolyn that the reason he didn't want to stop was because he was sure Sarah was angry with him for asking if Sammy could lead his mules again. He especially didn't want to talk about it in front of young Frank, who was staring up at him with a curious expression.

"I'd really like to spend the night in Walnutport," Carolyn persisted. "I miss Sarah and was hoping for the chance to visit with her."

The pleading look on his sister's face made Elias alter his decision. "Oh, all right. We'll spend the night in Walnutport and go to church there in the morning." *I just hope Sarah won't give me a cool reception.*

Chapter 27

On Sunday morning when Sarah entered the church with her children, she was surprised to see Patrick standing in the foyer talking to Pastor William. While she'd seen him in Sunday school a few times when they were children, she couldn't remember him ever coming to church since he'd become a man.

Sammy, Willis, and Helen gathered with a group of other children to visit, so Sarah headed over to say hello to Patrick.

"It's nice to see you here today," she said, joining him and the pastor.

"Figured it was the only way I'd get to—" Patrick halted his words, his face turning a light shade of red. "Uh . . . what I mean to say is, I figured it was about time I exposed myself to some religion." He looked over at Pastor William and grinned. "Sure don't want to end up like some of them rusty old canalers who only speak the Lord's name when they're mad about somethin'."

Pastor William's brows furrowed. "It's a shame to hear the way some of those men talk, and I'm hoping some of the services I'll be holding down at the canal will reach several of them for the Lord. Maybe some will seek Him this afternoon during the baptismal service we'll be having down there."

"I think I might like to attend that service," Patrick was quick to say.

"Are you planning to be baptized?" Sarah questioned.

Patrick shook his head. "Uh, no. Don't think I'm ready for anything like that."

"Well, let me know when you're ready to talk more about it." Pastor William glanced across the room. "I see Deacon Simms motioning to me, so if you two will excuse me, I'd better see what he wants."

When the pastor walked away, Patrick moved closer to Sarah. "Would you mind if I sit with you during church?"

Sarah hesitated but finally nodded. She didn't want people to get the wrong idea and think she and Patrick were courting, but she didn't want to discourage Patrick from coming to church again either.

Probably the best way for me to handle this, she decided, *is to put Helen on one side of me and Willis on the other. That will mean Patrick will have to sit beside Sammy.*

As Patrick sat on a blanket with Sarah and her children, sharing a picnic lunch after church, he was grateful that she'd invited him to join them. Not only was the fried chicken she'd prepared delicious, but he was finally getting a chance to visit with her. Of course, that was only when one of her kids wasn't blabbering about something he thought was unimportant. He couldn't believe that three little kids would have so much to talk about. Truth was, he wished they'd go off somewhere by themselves and play so he could talk to Sarah without any interruptions.

Just then, Patrick remembered the lollipops in his pocket. As soon as the kids were done eating their meal, he pulled the candy out and handed a red lollipop to Helen and the two orange ones to Willis and Sammy. "Here you go . . . a special treat from me," he said with a smile.

"Thanks!" Willis removed the wrapper and swiped his tongue over the lollipop.

Helen did the same. "Yum . . . good!"

Patrick looked over at Sammy and was rewarded with a scowl. "I hate orange. Ugh, it makes me sick!"

A wave of heat shot up the back of Patrick's neck. He remembered now that Mike had said Sammy liked cherry but didn't care for orange.

"Sorry about that. I really meant for the red one to be yours." Patrick looked over at Helen. "Would you trade your lollipop with your brother's?"

"No way!" Sammy shouted before Helen could

respond. "I ain't eatin' that after she's licked on it!"

"I'll tell you what," Patrick said, "I'll buy you another lollipop the next time I go to the store."

"Don't bother," Sammy muttered. "Oh look, there's Elias." He pointed across the way, scrambled to his feet, and dashed off.

"Oh look, there's Sarah," Carolyn said to Elias as they finished their picnic lunch. "I'd go over and talk to her, but it looks like she's kind of busy right now."

Elias glanced to the left and winced, feeling as if he'd been punched in the stomach. Sarah sat on a blanket next to Patrick. He knew he had no right to feel jealous, because he certainly had no claim on Sarah. But he couldn't help the urge he felt to go over there and tell Patrick to stay away from Sarah.

Carolyn rose to her feet. "I think I'll go talk to Sarah's sister, Kelly, awhile. She's sitting on the grass near the lock, sketching a picture. I'd like to see what it is."

Carolyn had just walked away when Sammy ran up to Elias and gave him a hug. "I'm glad you're here today! Why don't ya come over and sit on the blanket with us?"

"I don't think that's such a good idea," Elias said.

"Why not?"

"Your mother's visiting with Patrick, and I don't want to interrupt."

"I don't think she'd care." Sammy frowned. "Besides, if you go over, maybe Patrick will leave."

"I doubt that, but I'm curious. Why would you want Patrick to leave?"

Sammy wrinkled his nose. "He hangs around Mama all the time, and he says mean things to our dog."

Elias wasn't sure how to respond. It was clear that Sammy didn't care much for Patrick. The truth was, neither did he. One thing was clear: If Sarah was getting serious about Patrick, then Sammy might have to accept that fact whether he liked it or not.

Elias was about to suggest that he and Sammy go down to his boat so Sammy could meet Frank, who'd stayed on the boat with Ned, but Pastor William had just made the announcement that the baptismal service was about to begin.

"I'd better get ready to play along with the songs," Elias said, slipping the straps of his accordion over his arms and rising to his feet.

"Can I stand beside ya?" Sammy asked.

"Sure, that'd be just fine."

The pastor opened the service by leading the people in several lively songs. Elias enjoyed accompanying on his accordion, just as he'd done during church today, and Betsy, who'd apparently felt well enough to come, played along with her zither.

When the singing ended, Pastor William opened his Bible. "Proverbs 16:9 says, 'A man's heart deviseth his way: but the Lord directeth his steps.'" He smiled and stretched out his hands, as though encompassing the crowd. "Some folks think they know what's best, and they wander through life never asking God for direction. Some folks think they can do whatever they choose, and believe they don't need God at all."

Pastor William moved closer to the crowd. "In 1 Samuel 16:7, it says, 'The Lord seeth not as a man seeth; for man looketh on the outward appearance, but the Lord looketh on the heart.' We should all ask ourselves what the Lord sees when He looks on our hearts. Are we clean before the Lord, or does He see our sin—ugly and black?"

A hush fell over the crowd. No doubt everyone was taking to heart what the pastor had said.

"Before I begin baptizing, I want to invite any who haven't yet done so to confess their sins and accept Christ as their personal Savior."

To Elias's surprise, Ned, who'd obviously left the boat, stepped forward, lifted his gaze to the sky, and said, "Oh Lord, if You can care for a man as vile as me, then let it be so. I know I'm a sinner, and I ask You to forgive my sins and make me a new man."

Pastor William asked Ned to kneel before him,

and then he placed his hands on Ned's head and prayed for him. Then he guided the tearful canaler through a prayer of repentance. Following the prayer, the pastor explained that those who were about to be baptized would be following Christ's example, and that the act of baptism was an outward public showing of an inward faith. Finally, Ned and several others followed Pastor William into the canal, where he baptized each of them.

When Ned came out of the water, he wore a huge grin. "I'm now a clean vessel for my Master's use," he said, stretching his arms open wide. "I'm a changed man. My thoughts are different, and from this moment on, my actions will be different. I'm going to give up chewing tobacco, smoking cigarettes, swearing, and drinking. I'm going to try and live the way a Christian should."

Pastor William smiled, and then he reminded those who had been baptized that the Lord was stronger than the devil. "Remember, too," he said, "no matter what troubles come your way, never give up."

Elias pondered those words and realized that he needed to take them to heart. With all the troubles he'd had since he took over his grandfather's boat, he'd been on the verge of giving up several times. From now on, he was going to trust the Lord and take one day at a time.

Chapter 28

*O*n Monday morning, as Elias headed his boat in the direction of Easton, he was pleased to see how well Frank was doing with the mules. The boy had caught on quickly and didn't complain about a thing. With the exception of Sarah giving Elias the cold shoulder on Sunday while she became friendlier toward the blacksmith, things were looking up for Elias. He was quite sure that she was still angry with him for asking if Sammy could lead his mules.

"Hey, Ned," Bart Jarmon called as they passed his boat, going in the opposite direction, "I hear ya went for a dip in the canal yesterday."

Ned leaned over the boat and waved at Bart. "Found the Lord and got myself baptized, that's what I did!"

Bart leaned his head back and roared. "So you've done got religion now, huh?"

"That's right. I'm a new man in Christ, and I've given up chewin', cussin', smokin', and drinkin'. From now on, I'll be totin' a Bible everywhere I go."

Bart put his hands around his neck and coughed, like he was gagging. "Well, you'd better stay far away from me then, 'cause I sure don't want none of that holier-than-thou religious stuff rubbin' off on me."

"You'd be surprised how good you'd feel if ya confessed your sins and got right with God," Ned shouted in return.

Bart shook his head vigorously. "No thanks! I'm happy just the way I am."

As Bart's boat went past, Elias turned to Ned and said, "You handled that well, my friend. There was a day when I don't think you would have responded so nicely."

"That's true. I'd of shouted a few cuss words and waited until I saw Bart again, and then I'd have knocked his block clean off. Now I know it's best just to turn the other cheek."

Elias smiled. It was good to see such a positive change in Ned. Elias knew that his grandfather would have been pleased to see his old friend and helper witnessing to one of the other canalers.

Elias motioned to the tiller. "Would you mind steering the boat awhile? Carolyn's going to be washing some clothes soon, and I should go down there and see what I have that needs to be washed."

"Sure, boss, I'll do whatever ya ask."

"Thanks, I appreciate that." Elias thumped Ned on the back. "I shouldn't be gone too long."

When Elias went below, he found Carolyn in the galley, fumbling around in one of the cabinets.

"What are you looking for?" Elias asked.

"I thought I had two bars of that soap that floats, but there's only one in here now."

Elias frowned. "That's strange. Do you think you can get by with just the one until we stop at Cooper's store again?"

"I'm sure I can manage."

"How's your hand feeling?"

"Just fine."

"Are you sure you're up to washing clothes?"

She held up her hand. "It's almost as good as new, and it certainly won't hurt for me to get it wet."

"All right then. I'll go to my room and see what I have that needs to be washed."

"Ned gave me some of his clothes already, and Frank just had one shirt he said I could wash."

"I know. That poor boy and his family have been practically destitute since his father died. When Frank quits working for me at the end of the season I plan to see that he goes home with some money he can give his mother to help with expenses."

"You're a good man, Elias. I'm pleased to call you my brother."

He grinned. "I'm pleased to have you for a sister."

When Elias entered his cabin, he gathered up his dirty clothes, and then opened the drawer where he kept the pocket watch his grandfather had given him for his birthday several years ago.

"Now that's sure strange," he murmured when he saw that the watch wasn't there. *I wonder if I put it someplace else and forgot. Well, I don't have time to look for it right now, so hopefully I'll find it later on.*

"I'm going out to the garden to pull some carrots," Sarah told Hortence after they'd washed the breakfast dishes. "I want to do it before more boats come through."

"That's fine. I'll get started washing some clothes while you're in the garden."

"Thanks. Since the kids are playing upstairs in their rooms, the two of us should be able to get a lot done." Sarah smiled and hurried out the door.

When she stepped into the garden, she gasped. Not only were all of her cucumbers missing, but someone had taken most of her carrots. Everything had looked fine yesterday. This had to have happened sometime during the night or early this morning.

Sarah wondered if one of the mule drivers had come along and stolen the vegetables. It had happened before to several others who had gardens near the towpath.

She bent down and pulled six of the carrots that were still left, then turned toward the house. She was almost to the door when Kelly showed up.

"I haven't talked to you since Sunday, so I decided to come over and let you know that someone broke into our store and stole several things."

Sarah frowned. "I'm sorry to hear that. When did it happen?"

"We think it must have occurred either while we were in church, during the baptismal service, or sometime during the night."

Sarah pointed to her garden. "I wonder if it was the same person who stole from my garden."

Kelly folded her arms and tapped her foot. "It's always a concern when someone steals, especially when we don't know who it is, or if and when they might steal again."

"I know." Sarah frowned as she slowly shook her head. "Taking some things from my garden's a minor thing, but breaking into your store and stealing things is robbery. I hope that whoever did it will be caught and punished."

Chapter 29

A few weeks later, Elias decided to stop at Cooper's store to buy some more soap that floated, as well as several other items they were nearly out of. While he did the shopping, Ned and Frank waited on the boat, and Carolyn headed over to the lock tender's house to visit Sarah.

"It's nice to see you," Mike said when Elias entered the store. "How are things going?"

"Fairly well. I've got a new mule driver, and he's working out pretty good."

"Glad to hear it. I know Bobby was disappointed when he broke his leg and had to quit leading the mules."

"How's Bobby doing?" Elias asked. "I didn't get to see him the last time I was in Walnutport."

"He's getting along okay, but according to his aunt Martha, he's bored and doesn't like to sit around."

"Guess that's how it is with most kids."

"Yeah. My two never sit still." Mike chuckled. "From the looks of their rumpled bedsheets, I think they must keep moving even when they're sleeping."

Elias smiled. "How are things going here at the store? Is your business doing well?"

"It won't be if we keep getting broken into."

Elias's eyebrows shot up. "You had a break-in?"

Mike nodded. "It happened on the Sunday we were at the baptismal service. Whoever did it stole some groceries, as well as two of Kelly's paintings." Mike frowned. "The same day, Sarah had some vegetables taken from her garden, so we're thinking it might have been done by the same person who broke into our store."

"That's a shame. Any idea who might have done it?"

Mike drew in a quick breath and released it with a groan. "Here on the canal, we have so many poor folks, not to mention the rugged canalers who don't seem to have a conscience at all. It could have been most anyone, really."

"You're probably right."

"I'm always glad when any of the boatmen find the Lord, because then they give up their sinful lifestyle."

"I know I've seen a big change in my helper, Ned. He's not only given up his bad habits, but now he's begun witnessing to some of the other boatmen."

"That's good. Maybe if one of them's responsible for breaking into my store, they'll repent and won't do it again. And who knows . . . they might even make restitution." Mike shrugged. "I figure it was either done by one of the boatmen or maybe some desperate kid."

Elias thought about Carolyn's missing bar of soap and the pocket watch he hadn't been able to find, and wondered if Frank could be responsible. Might the boy have also stolen from Sarah's garden and broken into Mike's store? He did have an opportunity to do those things while Elias, Carolyn, and Ned were at the baptismal service that Sunday. He hated to think the boy would do such a thing, but knowing how poor Frank's family was, there was a chance that he might be the one. Elias debated about whether he should confront Frank and decided to wait for the right time to mention that things had been taken and then see if the boy acted guilty or owned up to it.

"It's so good to see you again," Sarah said, giving Carolyn a hug.

"It's good to see you, too. I've really missed our long talks."

"Same here. How's your hand feeling? Are the burns completely healed?"

Carolyn nodded. "I can't believe how well the salve worked that Dr. McGrath gave me."

"I'm glad. I know how miserable you were at first."

"Oh look, here comes that handsome blacksmith," Carolyn said, motioning to the kitchen window.

Sarah gulped. She hoped he wasn't coming to ask if she'd considered his marriage proposal. She wasn't ready to deal with that yet, and certainly not in front of Carolyn.

She hurried to the front door and opened it before Patrick had a chance to knock.

"Hello, Sarah. How are you?" he asked with a friendly grin.

"I'm fine. How are you?"

"Doin' all right." He shifted his weight from one foot to the other. "I need more bread . . . if you have some, that is."

"Yes, I do. If you'll wait right here, I'll get it for you." Sarah shut the door and hurried into the kitchen, leaving Patrick alone on the porch.

When she returned a few minutes later, she

handed him the bread and said, "It's fresh. I just baked it this morning."

"I'm sure it'll be real good." Patrick moved a bit closer. "I . . . uh . . . was wondering if—"

"I'm sorry. I can't visit with you right now because I have company inside."

"Who is it?"

"Elias's sister, Carolyn."

Patrick crooked an eyebrow. "Is Elias in there, too?"

"No, just Carolyn."

"That's good." Patrick's face flamed. "I mean, it's good you have some free time to visit with her."

"I don't get much free time for visiting, but traffic on the canal has been slower than usual today."

"Guess you may as well get used to it, because it probably won't be long and there won't be any boats hauling coal on the canal. The trains seem to be taking over more of that business all the time."

Sarah didn't need the reminder. Hardly a day went by that she didn't think about the future of the canal, which made her wonder how much longer she'd be able to support her children. If she could just save up enough money to open her own bakery, as Carolyn had suggested, all her problems would be solved.

"If you married me, you wouldn't have to work

so hard or worry about the future of the canal." He leaned closer. "What do you say, Sarah? Have you given it some thought?"

"I have thought about it, but I don't have an answer for you yet."

"When do you think you will?"

"I . . . I don't know. I'll need to pray about it some more and discuss it with my kids, of course."

"Oh." Patrick's brows furrowed. "Guess if it's left up to them, you'll say no 'cause I don't think any of 'em likes me too well."

"They need to get to know you better." Sarah glanced toward the house, wishing Patrick would go so she could continue her visit with Carolyn.

As if by divine intervention, the door opened, and Carolyn stepped out. "I'm sorry to interrupt, but Willis asked if he could take the dog out for a walk. Since Hortence is busy cleaning upstairs, I told him I'd have to ask you."

"I have no objection," Sarah said, "as long as he doesn't go far and stays right on the towpath."

"All right, I'll tell him." Carolyn smiled at Patrick. "I'm sure you'll enjoy that bread you're holding. Sarah's an excellent baker."

"Yeah, I know." Patrick stood for a moment, then mumbled, "Guess I'd better go."

"Good-bye, Patrick."

"See you at church on Sunday," he called as he headed in the direction of town.

When Patrick was a safe distance away, Sarah turned to Carolyn and said, "He asked me to marry him awhile back and wondered if I had an answer for him yet."

Carolyn's eyes widened. "What'd you tell him?"

"I said I'd need to think about it, pray about it, and discuss it with my kids."

"And have you?"

"I've thought about it, and prayed about it, but I haven't mentioned it to any of the kids."

"How come?"

"They don't like Patrick so well . . . especially Sammy, so I'm worried about how they might respond."

"Are you in love with Patrick?"

Sarah shook her head. "No, but I don't dislike him either."

"He seems to be a nice man, and he's very good-looking." Carolyn's cheeks turned pink. "Of course, that's just my opinion, although I don't know him very well."

Sarah sighed. "You're right, Patrick's good-looking and nice enough, but he's not—"

The front door swung open, and a yapping Bristle Face raced out the door with Willis on his heels. "Come back here you bad dog!" he shouted.

Bristle Face picked up speed, barking and growling as he ran along the edge of the canal. Sarah figured if the dog wasn't careful he might end up going for an unexpected swim.

In the next minute, Willis darted past Sarah, leaped for the dog, and landed with a splash in the canal!

"Help! Help! I can't swim!"

Chapter 30

*E*lias had left the store and was almost to the lock tender's house, when he heard a splash and someone hollering for help. That's when he spotted Willis, kicking, screaming, and gasping for air.

With his heart pounding like a blacksmith's anvil, Elias dropped his packages to the ground and raced down the towpath. "I'll get him!" he shouted to Sarah, who looked like she was about to jump into the canal.

Elias pulled off his boots, leaped into the water, and swam over to Willis. In one quick movement, he pulled the boy to his side. Using his free arm to swim, he brought Willis safely to shore.

With arms outstretched, Sarah dropped to her knees, reached for Willis, and pulled him to her chest. "Oh, thank the Lord you're all right!" Tears coursed down her cheeks, and then she and Willis both began to sob.

Instinctively, Elias squatted beside Sarah, wrapped his arms around her and Willis, and held them tightly. They sat like that for several minutes, until Elias felt someone touch his shoulder. He looked up and saw Carolyn smiling down at him.

"Thank God you came along when you did," she murmured. "You saved the boy's life."

Sarah pulled slowly away and nodded, apparently unable to speak.

Willis reached out to Elias and gave him another hug. "If ya hadn't jumped in the canal and grabbed holda me, I mighta died like my papa did."

The floodgates opened, and Sarah started sobbing again. Elias, unsure of what more he could do to calm Sarah down, looked up at Carolyn, hoping she could help.

"It's all right," Carolyn said, patting Sarah's shoulder. "Willis is safe now, and he seems to be fine."

When Sarah's sobbing finally subsided, Carolyn suggested they go inside. "Willis needs to get out of his wet clothes," she said.

"You're right." Sarah stood and took hold of Willis's hand. Then with a murmured, "Thank you, Elias," she hurried with her son toward the house.

Carolyn touched Elias's soggy shirtsleeve. "You'd better get back to the boat and change your wet clothes, too."

He gave a nod. "Although they'd probably dry on their own if I stayed out here in the hot sun awhile longer."

"I'll go inside and check on Sarah," Carolyn said. "Then I'll meet you on the boat."

Elias headed down the towpath to get the packages he'd dropped. He hoped Sarah would be okay. She'd looked so pale and shaken, and he wished there'd been more he could do. Well, at least he'd broken the ice with her, and he was glad she was speaking to him again.

After Sarah got Willis changed into some dry clothes, she went to her room and checked her appearance in the looking glass. She was shocked by the red blotches on her face, and the swollen look around her red-rimmed eyes made her appear as if she'd been crying for hours. She'd had a hard time getting control of her emotions and had continued to cry even while changing Willis's clothes. What if Elias hadn't come along when he did? She wasn't a strong swimmer, and Willis might have drowned if she'd jumped in and tried to save him. She would have done it, though. She would do whatever she could in order to save any of her children.

She thought about how secure she'd felt when Elias had put his arms around her and Willis. Even though she hadn't known Elias very long, she was strangely attracted to him.

Sarah gripped the edge of her dresser. *I can never give in to those feelings. I can never fall in love with a man who works on the canal.*

Thanks to the canal, she had lost her husband. She couldn't let it take one of her children, too.

She had to do something to get them away from the canal. Would marrying Patrick be the answer for her and the children?

Wo–o–o–o! Wo–o–o–o! The sound of a conch shell drove Sarah's thoughts aside. She'd have to think about their future later on. Right now, she had to get that stupid lock opened so another boat could come through.

Sarah dipped her hands into the washbasin she kept on her dresser, splashed some water on her face, and dried it with a towel. Then she hurried from the room and quickly made her way down the winding stairs.

She stopped in the parlor to check on the children, but they weren't there. She found them in the kitchen with Hortence and Carolyn, having cookies and milk.

"There's a boat coming," Carolyn said.

Sarah nodded. "I heard the conch shell blowing." She moved toward the door, calling over her shoulder, "Hortence, don't let any of my kids leave the house!"

"I won't," Hortence replied. "I'll keep them right here with me."

When Sarah stepped out the door, Carolyn followed. "I need to get back to Elias's boat so we can be on our way, but I wanted to make sure you were okay," she said, slipping her arm around Sarah's waist.

"I'll never be okay as long as we're living near

the canal. I need to find a better way of life for my kids." Sarah hurried toward the lock before Carolyn could respond.

When Carolyn returned to the boat, she found Elias in the galley, putting away the things he'd purchased at the store.

"How are Sarah and Willis doing?" he asked.

"Willis is fine. He and his sister and brother are sitting at Sarah's table eating cookies and drinking milk. It's Sarah I'm worried about. She was very upset when Willis fell in the canal."

Elias nodded. "I didn't know what to do or say to help calm her down."

"You saved her son's life, and she's very grateful."

He pulled his fingers through the back of his hair. "Yeah, but she still seemed upset when she went to the house."

"Of course she was. It was a shock when Willis fell in the canal. When Sarah came downstairs after helping the boy change his clothes, her face was red, and her eyes were swollen. I'm sure she did more crying after she went upstairs." The chair squeaked when Carolyn pulled it out and took a seat at the small table. "There's something else I think you should know."

"What's that?"

"The blacksmith asked Sarah to marry him, and I believe she's thinking about it."

Elias's forehead wrinkled, but then he shrugged. "If she loves him, then I wish them the best."

"But she doesn't love him. She's only considering his offer because she wants to get her children away from the canal."

"Guess that makes sense."

She shook her head. "No, it doesn't. I don't think Sarah should marry someone she doesn't love."

"Patrick seems like a nice-enough guy. Maybe she'll learn to love him."

Carolyn tapped her fingers along the edge of the table. "Maybe you should ask Sarah to marry you."

Elias's eyebrows shot up. "You're kidding, right?"

"No, I'm not. You love Sarah—I know you do. I can see the look of longing on your face when you talk about her, and there's a gentleness in your voice when you say her name."

"Okay, you're right; I do love Sarah. It's strange, though, because I haven't known her that long, but I began to have feelings for her soon after we met." He leaned against the cupboard and folded his arms. "I care about Sarah's children, too, and if I thought there was any chance at all that Sarah could love me in return, I might ask her to marry me. However . . ."

"You won't know if you don't ask. Why don't you go over there and talk to Sarah?"

"Now?"

"Yes, right now."

"I can't do that, Carolyn. We need to get moving up the canal."

She pursed her lips. "If you don't ask her now, it may be too late. She might accept Patrick's proposal."

Elias blinked a couple of times. "You think so?"

"I do."

"But what if she turns me down?" He touched the left side of his face. "What if she thinks I'm a fool for asking, when we've only known each other since the beginning of spring? What if she doesn't want to marry a man who looks like me?"

"You're too sensitive about the way you look, Elias. I've told you before that it's what's in a person's heart that counts." She placed her hand on his arm. "You really need to tell Sarah how you feel about her. If you don't, you'll always wonder if she could love you or not."

Elias drew in a deep breath and nodded slowly. "All right then, but I'd better do it quickly, before I lose my nerve."

Chapter 31

Sarah had just let a boat through the lock, and was about to enter the house, when Elias showed up. "How's Willis doing?" he asked.

"He's fine. Still a little shook up after falling into the canal."

"That's understandable." He leaned against the porch railing. "What about you, Sarah? Are you okay?"

She shrugged. "I'm doing as well as can be expected."

"I know it must have been frightening for you when Willis fell in, and I'm sure if I hadn't been there, you would have rescued him."

"I'm not a good swimmer, but I would have done my best. There have been so many accidents on this canal involving children, as well as adults. It scares me to think that one of my kids might get hurt or drown because I'm not able to be with them all the time." Sarah grimaced. "If I didn't have to be out here tending the lock, I could be a better mother to my kids."

Elias dipped his head, as though unable to look her in the eye. "I . . . uh . . . think I know a way that you could be with your children more."

"Oh?"

"You could marry me."

Sarah opened her eyes wide and sucked in her

breath. "I appreciate your concern, but I could never marry a man like you."

Elias's face flamed, and without another word, he whirled around and raced back to his boat.

"It was a stupid thing to do," Elias mumbled as he hurried toward his boat. "I should never have listened to Carolyn. I should have expected Sarah would respond that way. I will never open myself up to another woman!"

When Elias stepped onto the boat, Ned frowned and narrowed his eyes. "It's about time ya got back. Are we ever gonna get this boat goin'?"

"Don't start snapping at me," Elias shot back. "Need I remind you that I'm the captain of this boat?"

"Sorry, boss," Ned mumbled. "Guess I overstepped my bounds."

Elias, feeling more frustrated by the minute, leaned over the side of the boat and shouted at Frank: "Get those mules moving now; I'm ready to go!"

Ned hurried to pull up the gangplank, and soon the boat was moving toward the lock.

"Take over the tiller, would you, Ned?" Elias stepped aside. "I need to go below for a few minutes."

"Sure thing, boss." Ned took Elias's place, and Elias hurried below, unable to bear the thought of seeing Sarah again.

He found Carolyn in the galley, peeling potatoes and carrots. "How'd it go with Sarah?" she asked with a hopeful expression.

"She said she would never marry a man like me." He touched the side of his face. "I told you she was bothered by my birthmark, and I guess I can't really blame her. Who'd want to be seen with a man who bears an ugly red blotch on his face?"

Carolyn stopped peeling and turned to face Elias. "I'm sure Sarah's not bothered by your birthmark."

"Yes, she is. She was looking right at the mark on my face when she said she could never marry a man like me."

"Are you sure about that? Did you ask her what she meant by that?"

"There was no point in asking when I already knew."

"Maybe you should go back there and ask—just to be sure you didn't misunderstand."

He shook his head determinedly. "We need to get going. We've lost enough time in Walnutport as it is. Ned's steering the boat into the lock right now."

"But what if Sarah marries Patrick?"

He shrugged. "What Sarah does is none of my business. As far as I'm concerned, I never want to see her again!"

Chapter 32

"*I* want to stop and see Sarah," Carolyn said to Elias as they approached the Walnutport lock several weeks later.

"What for?"

"Since you'll be dropping me off in Easton so I can get things ready for the new school year, this will be my last opportunity to say good-bye to Sarah. Besides, I need to go into Cooper's store and get that painting Kelly's been holding for me. It's the one of the rainbow that I want to give Mother for her birthday next month."

"Okay, but I don't want to spend a lot of time here. After Ned takes us through the lock, we'll dock near Cooper's store and I'll go inside to get the picture while you go over to Sarah's." He rubbed his chin. "Probably should pick up a few supplies I'm needing, too."

"Wouldn't you like to see Sarah?"

Elias shook his head. "Right now, I'm going below, just like I've done whenever we've gone through the Walnutport lock these last several weeks."

Carolyn placed her hand on his arm. "I wish you'd reconsider and see Sarah with me."

"I'm not going, and I'd appreciate it if you didn't keep asking."

"Okay," Carolyn mumbled. "Would you tell the Coopers I said good-bye?"

"Sure." Elias turned and tromped down the stairs. When he entered his cabin, his nose twitched at the musty odor. He ought to be getting used to it by now, but the lingering smell still bothered him.

He dropped to his knees and reached under his bunk for the tin can where he kept his money, but felt nothing. "Now, that's sure strange," he muttered.

He flattened his body closer to the floor and peered under the bunk, feeling around with his hands. The can was missing!

Elias's heartbeat picked up speed. Despite further searching, he still hadn't found his pocket watch, and now his money was missing, too. Someone had obviously been in his cabin and taken these things. The question was, who?

When Elias was sure the boat had gone through the lock, he went up to the main deck, finally ready to confront Frank about his missing things.

"Pull the boat over near Cooper's store," Elias told Ned. "Carolyn's getting off so she can visit Sarah, and I've got some business with Frank."

"Sounds good. Think I'll go into the store and get some root beer," Ned said. "Will you be doing some shopping there today?"

"I'd planned to, but since I can't find my money . . ."

Ned's bushy eyebrows shot up. "You lost your money?"

"I'll explain things later." Elias moved over to where Carolyn stood near the bow of the boat. "Would you have some money I could borrow for the supplies I need? I seem to have misplaced my can of money." He didn't want to frighten Carolyn by telling her he thought his things had been stolen.

"I'd be happy to loan you some money." Carolyn went below and returned a few minutes later with an envelope. "Here you go," she said, handing it to Elias. "Take as much as you need."

"Thanks."

"Do you need me to help you look for your money?" she asked.

"That's all right. I'm sure it'll turn up." *It had better turn up,* he thought grimly.

"Okay." She lifted the edge of her gingham dress and stepped onto the gangplank Ned had set in place. "I shouldn't be at Sarah's too long, and I'll meet you back here when I'm done."

As soon as Carolyn left, Elias hurried off the boat. "I need to speak to you," he said, joining Frank, where he stood several feet off the towpath, feeding the mules.

"Sure, what's up?" the boy asked.

"Several weeks ago, Cooper's store was robbed. Do you know anything about that?"

Frank shook his head. "Just heard some talk about it, that's all."

Elias rested his arm against a nearby tree. "The

same day the store got robbed, I discovered that my pocket watch was also missing. Then a short time ago, I went to my cabin to get my money, but the can I keep it in is missing, too. Would you know anything about that?"

"No, sir. I've never seen your pocket watch, and I don't know nothin' about your money neither."

"There were some things taken from Sarah's garden the same day as the store was robbed. Would you know anything about that?"

The boy's face colored, and he hung his head. "I . . . I did snitch some of her carrots 'cause I was hungry, but that's all I ever took." He lifted his head and looked at Elias with a sober expression. "Maybe you oughta ask Ned about your missin' things. He's on the boat most of the time, so he's had more of a chance to sneak into your cabin and take stuff than I have."

Elias debated what to do. Ned had changed since his conversion, and even before that, as far as Elias knew, Ned had never stolen anything from him or his grandfather. Elias wondered how Ned would respond if he questioned him about this.

He placed his hand on Frank's shoulder. "I'm going to trust that what you've told me is true, but from now on, if you're hungry or need something, I want you to tell me."

"Okay."

"And no more taking things from Sarah's or anyone else's garden. Is that clear?"

"Yes, sir."

"Good boy." Elias turned and headed for Cooper's store.

When Hortence let Carolyn into Sarah's house, she informed her that Sarah was upstairs in her room.

"Is she taking a nap?" Carolyn questioned.

"I don't think so. She said she was going up there to look for something in her trunk." Hortence motioned to the stairs. "Why don't you go on up? I'm sure she'll be glad to see you."

Carolyn hurried up the stairs. When she saw that Sarah's door was shut, she rapped lightly on it.

"Come in," Sarah called.

Carolyn entered the room and found Sarah standing in front of her looking glass, wearing a beautiful, ivory-colored dress with a high neckline and puffed sleeves.

"What a pretty dress," Carolyn murmured. "You look lovely in it."

Sarah whirled around. "Oh, Carolyn, it's so good to see you." She moved quickly across the room and gave Carolyn a hug.

"I'm heading back to Easton to get ready for the new school year," Carolyn said. "I asked Elias to stop in Walnutport so I could come here and say good-bye."

"I'm sorry you have to go. Do you think you might be back next summer?"

"I don't know. I guess it all depends on whether Elias still has his boat."

"Why wouldn't he have it? Is he thinking about selling it?"

"I'm not sure; he hasn't said anything about that. But even if I don't come to Walnutport again, maybe you can visit me in Easton sometime."

Sarah shook her head. "As long as I'm stuck here on the canal, I won't be able to visit anywhere."

"Maybe this winter, when the canal's closed."

"We'll have to wait and see how it goes."

Carolyn had a hunch the reason for Sarah's hesitation was because of her financial situation. She probably didn't have the money to make the trip to Easton by train, and with the canal closing down during the winter, catching a ride on one of the boats was out of the question. Even hiring a driver to take them by horse and carriage would be costly.

Carolyn was tempted to offer to pay Sarah and the children's way to Easton, but didn't want to offend her, so she changed the subject.

"Now about that beautiful dress you're wearing . . . Please don't tell me it's a wedding dress and that you've decided to marry Patrick O'Grady."

"It is a wedding dress, but not for a marriage to Patrick." Sarah shook her head. "I still haven't made a decision on that. I think I'm going to wait until the end of boating season to make any decisions about my future."

"That's probably a wise decision. You wouldn't want to make a mistake about something you'll have to live with for the rest of your life."

Tears welled in Sarah's eyes as her fingers traced the edge of the collar on her dress. "If Sam were still alive, today would have been our tenth wedding anniversary." She sniffed. "I thought it might make me feel closer to him if I tried the dress on today, but it's only made me feel weepy."

"I'm sure you still miss him."

Sarah nodded. "Some days more than others, but as time goes on, the pain lessens."

Carolyn stared out Sarah's bedroom window at the puffy white clouds floating past. She wanted to talk to Sarah about Elias but wasn't sure how to begin.

"Where are your thoughts taking you?" Sarah asked. "You look like you're someplace else right now."

"I . . . uh . . . was thinking about my brother."

"How's Elias doing? His boat has come through the lock several times in the last few weeks, but I haven't seen him even once, and I—well, I've really missed him."

"He's been staying below in his cabin, while Ned steers the boat."

"All the time?"

"No, just when he goes through the Walnutport lock."

"What's the reason for that?"

Carolyn drew in a quick breath. "He's been avoiding you."

"Is it because I turned down his unexpected marriage proposal?"

"Yes. No. Well, that's only part of the reason."

Sarah tipped her head. "I don't understand."

"Elias was deeply hurt when you said you could never marry a man like him. He thinks you turned him down because of his birthmark—because it's ugly, and you can't bear to look at it."

Sarah shook her head. "That's not true. I've never minded Elias's birthmark. The reason I said I could never marry a man like him is because he's a boatman." Sarah took a seat on the edge of her bed and motioned for Carolyn to do the same.

"From the time I was a young girl, I vowed never to marry a canaler," Sarah continued.

"Why's that?"

"I'd seen how hard Mama worked on Papa's boat, with little or no appreciation, and both my sister and I were expected to lead Papa's mules, walking long hours every day with no pay at all. Papa kept all the money we should have earned." Sarah released a lingering sigh. "I ran away with Sam, and we got married just so we could both get away from the canal. Then later, when we ended up coming back to Walnutport and he began tending the lock, I was faced with a different problem."

"What problem was that?"

"Fear. I became fearful that something bad would happen to my husband or one of my kids because we lived so close to the canal. Sure enough, the canal took Sam, and if not for Elias, it might have taken Willis, too." Tears welled in Sarah's eyes as she slowly shook her head. "So you see why I could never marry a boatman or anyone else who works on the canal."

"I'm glad you explained all this. Now I just have one more question to ask before I go."

"What's that?"

"Do you care for my brother?"

Sarah nodded. "Yes, I do. Even though I haven't known him very long, his kindness and gentle spirit have touched my heart deeply. If Elias wasn't a boatman, I would have accepted his proposal."

Carolyn took hold of Sarah's hand and gave her fingers a gentle squeeze. "Thanks for sharing from your heart. It gives me a better understanding of things." She rose from the bed. "I don't want to keep Elias waiting, so I'd better go. I'll write to you when I get to Easton, and I hope you'll write to me."

"Yes, I will."

Carolyn gave Sarah one final hug; then she hurried out the door. She needed to speak with Elias right away.

Chapter 33

"Can I talk to you a minute?" Elias asked Ned, when he found him sitting on a rock near the canal with his fishing line cast into the water.

"Yeah, sure. What's up?"

Elias lowered himself to the ground beside Ned. "I know you're aware of the break-in that occurred at Cooper's store several weeks back."

"Uh-huh."

"And you knew that someone had also taken some things from Sarah's garden that day."

Ned nodded. "That's nothin' new around here, though. People steal stray chickens and snitch things from the gardens along the towpath all the time." He offered Elias a sheepish grin. "Not that it's right, of course."

"No, it's certainly not, and neither is stealing from me."

Ned's bushy eyebrows furrowed. "What are ya talkin' about?"

"My pocket watch came up missing around the same time as Cooper's store got robbed, and now my money's also missing."

"Maybe you misplaced them."

Elias shook his head. "No. I've been keeping the money in a tin can underneath my bunk, and it's not there."

"Do ya think Frank might have taken it? I

mean, the kid's family is poor as a church mouse."

"I asked the boy about it before I went to Cooper's store."

"What'd he say?"

"He said he hadn't stolen anything from me."

"And ya believe him?"

Elias shrugged. "I've no reason not to believe him."

"Have ya looked in the boy's cabin?"

"Yes, I did that right after I spoke to him, but there was no sign of my watch or the money. I've looked pretty much everywhere on the boat—everywhere except for your quarters, that is."

Ned's forehead wrinkled deeply. "I hope ya don't think I had anything to do with it." His face turned red as he pulled his fishing line in with a jerk. "Before I became a Christian, I had lots of bad habits, but other than a few vegetables and chickens I took when I was a kid, I've never stolen anything in my life!"

Elias placed his hand on Ned's shoulder. "Calm down. You're getting yourself worked up for nothing. I wasn't accusing you of taking my things. I was just going to ask if you knew anything about it."

Ned shrugged Elias's hand away. "If I knew anything, don'tcha think I'd woulda told ya about it right away?"

Elias's face heated. "Well, I hope that you would."

"Did ya have anything missin' before ya hired Frank to lead the mules?"

"No, but—"

Ned clapped his hands. "There ya go! He's the one who done it, and I don't care what he says."

Elias drew in a deep breath and released it with a groan. "Since I have no proof that he stole anything, I suppose I'll have to take him at his word."

"Take who at his word?" Carolyn asked, touching Elias's shoulder.

He whirled around. "Oh, I didn't realize you were back."

She gave a nod. "I just got here and heard you talking about taking someone at his word."

"I was talking about Frank."

"What about him?"

Elias told Carolyn about the conversation he'd had with Frank.

"He accused me of it just now," Ned spoke up.

Elias shook his head. "I did not accuse you. I just—"

"It makes no never mind. The money's gone, and I think Frank took it." Ned rose to his feet. "The fish ain't bitin' today. Think I'll wait for you on the boat."

When Ned left, Carolyn took a seat on the rock where he'd been sitting. "Do you think Frank was telling the truth about not taking your things?" she asked Elias.

He shrugged. "I've got no proof that he did, so

unless and until I do, I'll have to give him the benefit of the doubt." Elias started to rise, but she placed her hand on his arm.

"There's something I need to tell you."

"What's that?"

"It's about what Sarah told me while I was at her house, saying good-bye."

He frowned. "I'm not interested in anything she has to say."

"I think you will be when you hear what it is."

"I doubt it."

"Elias, please let me tell you what she said."

He folded his arms and stared straight ahead. "Go ahead, if you must."

"When I told Sarah how upset you were over her saying she could never marry a man like you, she said—"

"You discussed my feelings with Sarah?" Elias's jaw clenched so tightly that his teeth ached.

"Well, yes, and—"

"How could you, Carolyn? How could you even think of talking to Sarah about my reaction to her rejection of me?"

"Since you were so upset about it, I thought she had the right to know."

He shook his head. "Sarah doesn't care how I feel."

"Yes, she does, and she wasn't referring to the red mark on your face when she said she could never marry a man like you."

"What was she referring to?"

"She was talking about the fact that you're a boatman."

"You mean she'd be ashamed to be married to a boatman?"

"Not ashamed. Fearful."

"Of what?"

"That the canal might take you or one of her children the way it did her husband. She's also afraid that if she married a boatman, one of her children might be forced to become a mule driver, the way she and her sister were when they were girls."

Elias slapped his hand against his pant leg. "That's ridiculous! I'd never force Sarah's children or any children we might have of our own to lead my mules."

"That's good to hear. Why don't you tell Sarah that?"

He shook his head. "If she's fearful of the canal and doesn't want to be married to a boatman, then I doubt she'd change her mind about marrying me."

"She might if she knew how much you loved her and if you gave her your word that you'd never make any of the children lead your mules."

Elias sat silently, mulling things over.

"If you don't do something soon, it might be too late."

"What's that supposed to mean?"

"Patrick's still after Sarah to marry him, and she plans to give him her answer by the time the canal closes for the winter."

"That's a few months away."

"Yes, but she might make her decision sooner, and if she chooses him, it'll be too late for the two of you."

"She'd probably be better off with Patrick than me."

"Why do you say that?"

"He's handsome and doesn't work on the canal."

"But if she doesn't love him . . ."

"It doesn't matter. Sarah won't marry me as long as I'm a boatman." Elias jumped up. "We need to get back on the boat. It's time we headed for Easton."

"Did you get the painting and tell the Coopers good-bye for me?"

"Yes, and I'm sure Mother will be very happy with her birthday present."

Carolyn sighed. "I wish we didn't have to go. I wish we could stay right here and enjoy the sunshine and warm breeze blowing off the water."

"Well, we can't. I need to get to Easton, and so do you."

Chapter 34

*T*hroughout the month of September, Elias avoided Sarah. He'd been thinking about the things Carolyn had told him but wasn't sure what, if anything, he should do. If Sarah wouldn't marry him because he was a boatman, then even if he spoke to her about marriage again, she wouldn't change her mind. Yet if he didn't speak to her about it, she might end up marrying the blacksmith. Still, if Sarah wasn't going to give Patrick an answer until the canal closed for the winter, Elias had some time to decide what he should do.

Carolyn had also mentioned that she'd suggested to Sarah the idea of opening a bakery in town, but Sarah had said she didn't have the money for that. Elias felt bad that Sarah had to work so hard and struggle financially. If she married Patrick, she wouldn't have to worry about either of those things anymore.

"Ya look like you're a million miles from here," Ned said, joining Elias at the bow of the boat. "Whatcha thinkin' about anyway?"

"Nothing much." *Nothing I wish to talk about.*

Ned tipped his head back and sniffed the air. "Fall's definitely here. Can ya smell the musty odor from the leaves that have fallen on the ground?"

Elias gave a quick nod.

"Won't be long, and the canal will be closin' down for the season. Got any idea what you'll do durin' the winter months?"

"I haven't figured that out yet."

"Well, you'd better figure somethin' out soon, 'cause both of the boardin' houses in town fill up real quick with the boatmen who've got no homes of their own, and word has it that one of the boardin' houses might be up for sale, so that one could be gone by winter."

"I hear that some of the canalers live on their boats during the winter months."

"Yep, that's true. Think ya might do that?"

Elias shrugged. "Right now my plan is to stop at Cooper's store as soon as we get to Walnutport so I can pick up some supplies. Then we'll push on and get our load of coal picked up in Mauch Chunk before the end of the day."

"Ya still want me to steer the boat when we head into the lock at Walnutport?"

"Yes, I'll stay below until we get through, and then, unless you need something from the store, you can stay on the boat and keep an eye on things while I go in."

"Don't need a thing this time." Ned clicked his tongue noisily as he shook his head. "Sure don't make sense to me the way ya hide out below every time we go through that lock. Ya don't do it at the other locks we go through."

Elias gripped the tiller until his fingers ached. He wished Ned would stop plying him with questions—especially questions he'd rather not answer.

When Elias entered Cooper's store, he found Mike sweeping up some broken glass near the front window.

"What happened?" Elias asked.

Mike frowned. "Sometime during the night, someone broke into the store again. This time, they took even more items than before."

"That's a shame. Do you think it was done by the same person who broke in the other time?"

"I'm not sure, but I wouldn't be surprised."

"Several weeks ago someone stole something from me, too."

"Really? What'd they steal?"

"A can of money I had hidden in my cabin."

"Did they leave any clues?"

Elias shook his head.

"Well, they left one here." Mike reached under the front counter and produced a faded piece of blue material. "I found this stuck to a chunk of the glass that was still in the store window. I'm guessin' it came off the thief's shirt when he crawled through the window."

Elias pursed his lips. "Hmm . . . There's nothing unusual about the color of the material. I suppose it could belong to most anyone."

"But here's something interesting. Look at this." Mike pointed to a blotch of blood on the material. "Whoever came in through the window must have cut his arm on the broken glass."

Elias studied the material. "That's definitely a clue—or at least it would be if we knew who in the area had a cut on his arm." Whew! At least he knew for sure that it hadn't been Frank or Ned. They were definitely not here last night, and neither of them had a cut on their arm. "Have you looked around outside for any clues? It rained yesterday, so maybe the thief left some footprints."

"No, I haven't looked. Let's go see."

Elias followed Mike out the door. Sure enough, a pair of large footprints led to the window of the store.

"So we know it was a man," Mike said as they returned to the store. "Only trouble is there are a lot of men in the area with big feet."

"Have you notified the sheriff?"

"Not yet. I was going to do that as soon as Kelly had time to mind the store for me so I could go to town."

Elias was about to say that he would tell the sheriff, when the door opened and burly Bart Jarmon stepped in.

"Came to get a few supplies I didn't realize I still needed," he said, looking at Mike.

"That's fine," Mike replied. "Look around the store and get whatever you need."

Bart headed down one of the aisles and returned a few minutes later with several items, which he placed on the counter.

"That'll be ten dollars," Mike said after he'd added up Bart's purchases.

Bart reached into his pants pocket. As he fumbled, trying to get his money, a gold pocket watch fell out and landed on the floor.

Elias gasped. It was his missing watch—the one Grandpa had given him.

"Where'd you get that?" he asked Bart.

Bart's face colored as he bent to pick it up. "Found it. Can't remember where, though."

"Can I take a look at it?"

"What for?"

"I had a pocket watch like that, but it's missing."

Bart quickly stuck the watch back in his pocket. "What are ya sayin'? Are ya accusin' me of takin' your watch?" He squinted his beady eyes and glared at Elias.

Mike moved closer to Bart and pointed to the bandage sticking out from under the man's rolled-up shirtsleeve. Elias hadn't noticed it until now.

"What happened to your arm?" Mike asked.

The crimson color in Bart's face darkened, and rivulets of sweat beaded up on his forehead. "I . . . uh . . . cut myself on a piece of metal."

Mike looked over at Elias, then back at Bart. "Someone broke into my store last night, and I'm sure whoever did it cut their arm on the broken

236

glass in the front window. You wouldn't know anything about that, would you?"

Bart's eyes narrowed as he shook his head. "And you've got no proof that I do."

"Maybe we ought to take a look around your boat," Elias spoke up. "Just to be sure you're telling the truth."

"I think that's an excellent idea," Mike agreed.

Bart shifted nervously and pulled his fingers through the sides of his dark, bushy hair. "There's no need for that—no need a'tall."

"Why's that, Bart?" Mike questioned.

Bart started edging toward the door, but Mike moved quickly to block it. Elias, his heart hammering in his chest, jumped in front of the door, too.

Bart scowled at them. "Get outa my way! Ya can't keep me here, ya know!"

Mike planted his hands on his hips and stared at Bart. "Then tell us what you know about the break-in here at my store."

Bart put up his fists like he was ready for a fight, but Mike didn't back down.

Elias had never been one for violence and didn't know what he'd do if Bart started swinging. He sure couldn't let Mike, who was several inches shorter and weighed a lot less than Bart, do battle with the brute alone. On the other hand, Elias wasn't sure how successful he and Mike would be, even if they both took Bart on. A man like

Bart, whose breath smelled of liquor, might be a lot stronger than the two of them put together.

"All right, I'm the one," Bart blurted, staring at Mike with a look of defiance. "I broke into your store twice and woulda done it again if I'd run outa money." His gaze swung to Elias. "And yes, I came aboard your boat when you were docked here so you could attend one of them Bible-thumpin' preacher's meetings, and I stole your pocket watch and a bar of that white soap that floats. Then later, when you was docked near one of the stores in Mauch Chunk, I took the can of money."

White-hot anger welled in Elias's chest, and he had to take a couple of deep breaths to calm down. "Why, Bart? What made you do such a terrible thing?"

"I'd like to know that myself," Mike put in.

Bart took a step back and leaned against the counter. "Things have been bad for me lately, and I was afraid I might lose my boat."

"How come? What's happened?" Mike wanted to know.

"I spent most of my money on liquor and gambling, and if I hadn't done somethin' quick, I'da been headed for the poorhouse."

"Stealing other people's property is not the answer," Elias said. " 'Thou shalt not steal' is one of God's commandments."

Bart slammed his left fist into his right hand. "I

don't give a hoot nor a holler 'bout God's commandments! I live by my own rules. Have ever since I was a boy and my old man ran off and left me, Ma, and my three sisters alone to fend for ourselves."

"I understand you've had a hard life," Mike said, "but stealing's against the law, and now you'll have to go with us to see the sheriff."

Bart shook his head vigorously. "Uh-uh, no way! I'd rather die than go to jail." Bart lowered his head and barreled right between Mike and Elias, nearly knocking them off their feet. He jerked open the front door and dashed outside.

As soon as Mike and Elias regained their balance, they ran out the door after him.

Elias could see Bart up ahead, racing down the path in the opposite direction of town.

A wagon pulled by two horses came out of nowhere. When Bart ran in front of it, the horses spooked and reared up. One of the horses struck Bart in the head, and he fell to the ground.

By the time Mike and Elias caught up to the scene of the accident, the driver of the wagon was on his knees beside Bart, shaking his head.

"He ran in front of me before I even knew what had happened," the man said, looking at Mike.

Blood oozed from Bart's head, and he didn't appear to be breathing.

Elias knelt down and felt for a pulse, but there was none. He looked up at Mike and slowly shook his head. "Bart's dead, and what a tragedy. Life is so short, and to waste it the way he did is a real shame."

"Yes," Mike agreed, "and now Bart's life is over, and he'll never have a chance to make restitution for what he did. Bart's last words to us were that he'd rather die than go to jail. It's sad to say, but the poor lost soul got his wish."

As Elias and his crew headed up the canal toward Mauch Chunk, he kept thinking about Bart and everything that had transpired after he'd been killed. Mike had gone to town to get the sheriff, as well as the undertaker, while Ned and Elias had searched Bart's boat for evidence. They'd not only found several items that had been taken from Mike's store, but also Elias's can, with what was left of his money. Of course, Elias had retrieved his watch from Bart's pocket before he'd boarded the man's boat.

"I'm going down to my cabin to put my money away," Elias told Ned. "Would you take over the tiller for me?"

"Sure thing, boss." Ned offered Elias a wide grin. "Sure am glad ya got some of your money back."

"So am I, but I wish it could have been under better circumstances."

Ned nodded solemnly. "Yeah, it's too bad about Bart. Wish he coulda found the Lord and turned his life around before he died."

"There are too many like Bart in our world," Elias said. "That's why we, who are Christians, should take every opportunity to witness to others about the Lord—not only through our words, but by our deeds."

"Yep, you're right, and that's just what I'm aimin' to do."

Elias thumped Ned's back. "I'm going below now, but I shouldn't be long."

When Elias entered his cabin, he decided that he needed to find a better hiding place for his money than under his bunk. He thought about putting it inside one of the small cabinets in the room, but figured that'd be one of the first places someone would look.

He glanced around, taking in every detail of the small, dimly lit cabin. Finally, his gaze came to rest on the old trunk sitting at the foot of his bunk. It had been Grandpa's trunk, where he'd kept his clothes and possibly a few other things. Elias had been meaning to go through it but just hadn't taken the time.

Maybe I could hide my money at the bottom of the trunk, he thought. *If someone should open it, they'll think it's just a trunk full of clothes.*

Elias knelt on the floor and opened the lid of the trunk; then he reached inside and removed a stack of clothes—shirts, trousers, and Grandpa's old straw hat.

He spotted something black and reached inside

again. When he pulled it out, he realized it was Grandpa's Bible.

A lump formed in his throat. Many an evening when Elias and Grandpa had been on the boat together, Grandpa had shared several passages from the Bible.

Elias slid his fingers along the edge of the leather cover; then he opened the Bible to a place where a piece of paper stuck out. He quickly discovered that it was a letter that had been written to him:

Dear Elias,

After I'm gone, my boat will belong to you. It's yours to do with as you choose. I love this old boat, and it's given me many good years, but I know it won't be long before the canal era comes to a close. So if you decide not to captain the boat yourself, you're free to sell it, and then you can use the money to buy whatever you like.

Tears welled in Elias's eyes as he stared at the letter. *If Grandpa really meant what he said, then I have a decision to make. Should I keep the boat going for as long as I can, or sell it and find something else to do?*

Chapter 35

"*H*ow come we haven't seen Elias in so long?" Sammy asked Sarah one morning in early October.

"I'll bet he comes by when you're in school." Willis poked Sammy's arm with his bony elbow. "Besides, he don't stop to say hi to us no more, anyhow." He looked at Sarah. "Is Elias mad at you, Mama?"

Sarah blinked. "Now what made you ask such a question?"

" 'Cause once I heard Uncle Mike say that Ned told him Elias hides out on his boat when he comes through the lock so he don't have to see you."

Sarah cringed. For some time, ever since she'd turned down Elias's marriage proposal, Ned had been the one steering the boat whenever it came through her lock. *Maybe Elias is still upset with me for turning down his marriage proposal. I hope Carolyn explained my reasons to him. I hope he understands.*

Willis tugged on Sarah's sleeve. "Is Elias ever comin' to see us again? Is he, huh?"

"I don't know, son." She pointed to his bowl of mush. "Hurry now and finish your breakfast. Hortence will be here any minute, and I'd like us to have the dishes cleared away before she arrives."

"I hope Elias is at church this Sunday," Sammy said. "I sure do miss him."

I miss him, too, Sarah thought with regret. Her gaze came to rest on the letter she'd placed on the counter. It was from Carolyn and had arrived yesterday at Mike's store, which also served as the local post office. Carolyn had told Sarah some interesting things about Easton and mentioned how things were going with the students in her class. But she'd made no mention of Elias at all.

Willis nudged Sarah's arm. "Sure hope that mean blacksmith's not at church this time. I don't like it when he sits on the pew between us, Mama."

"Patrick is not mean. He's a nice man, and you shouldn't talk about him that way," Sarah said with a shake of her head.

"He's mean to Bristle Face," Helen spoke up. "I seen him kick at our dog once when you wasn't lookin'."

Sarah flinched. Even after all these months of Patrick coming around, the children—and the dog—still didn't care for him. She hadn't given him an answer to his proposal yet, and with the children feeling the way they did, she didn't know what to do. Would things be better for them if she married Patrick? Would the children learn to accept him as their stepfather?

Sarah took a sip of her tea and contemplated

things further. *If I don't marry Patrick, how will I get my family away from the canal?*

She didn't have near enough money saved up in order to open her own bakery and she might never have enough. With winter coming, the only money she'd make would be from the bread she planned to sell in Mike and Kelly's store. As far as she could tell, her family's future looked hopeless. Maybe her only choice was to marry Patrick.

A knock sounded on the door, and a few seconds later, Hortence entered the kitchen.

"You don't have to knock every time you come over," Sarah said, smiling at Hortence. "You're like one of the family now."

Hortence smiled in return. "I realize that, but as Mother always says, 'You don't want to ever forget your manners.' " She motioned to the table. "I see you're still eating breakfast. I must be early this morning."

Sarah shook her head. "You're not early. We've just spent more time visiting than usual."

"We was talkin' about Patrick and how much he hates our dog," Willis said.

"Before that it was Elias we was talkin' about," Sammy added.

Hortence pulled out an empty chair at the table and sat down. "Speaking of Elias, did you know that he sold his boat and left the canal?"

Sarah's mouth opened wide. "He did?"

"That's right. Mother heard it from Mavis Jennings, and Mavis said she heard it from Freda Miller."

"Where'd Elias go?" A sense of sadness settled over Sarah like a heavy blanket of fog. "Did he move back to Easton?"

Hortence shrugged. "I'm not sure. I just know he's gone."

Sammy jumped up, nearly knocking over his glass of milk. "That's not fair! If Elias sold his boat and went away, we'll never see him again!" Tears welled in his eyes, and he started pacing.

"Calm down, Sammy. You're getting yourself all worked up." The truth was, Sarah felt pretty worked up herself, but she couldn't let the children or Hortence know that. Oh, how she wished things could have worked out for her and Elias, but under the circumstances, it was probably for the best that he was gone. If he'd stayed any longer, she might have weakened and changed her mind about marrying him. For her children's sake, she couldn't allow that to happen—not with him being a boatman.

Sammy stopped pacing and stomped his foot. "Wish I knew where Elias was. If I did, I'd go after him!"

Sarah reached out and pulled him to her side. "Elias must have had a reason for leaving. We need to accept his decision."

"Maybe he went back to Easton to work in his

father's newspaper office," Hortence said. "Hauling coal up the canal means long, hard days, and he probably got tired of it."

Sammy cast Sarah an imploring look. "Can we go to Easton and see if he's there? Can we ask him to come back here, Mama?"

Sarah blinked against the tears clouding her vision. "No, son. We need to let him go."

"But I love Elias, and was hopin' he'd be our new papa someday."

Sarah's heart felt as if it would break in two. "It's not meant to be. Someday, if it's God's will, I might get married again."

At that moment, Sarah made a decision. As soon as she saw Patrick again she would give her answer to his proposal.

As Patrick headed for Sarah's place, he thought about what he was going to say to her. He'd given Sarah several months to make up her mind, and he was tired of waiting. Well, she'd better give him an answer today, or he might tell her to forget it. Sarah wasn't the only fish in the canal, and if she didn't want him, he was sure he could find someone who did.

He stepped onto her porch and rapped on the door. When it opened, Willis stood there with that scruffy terrier, who immediately began to bark and growl.

"Can I speak to your mama?" Patrick asked the

boy, making sure he was talking loud enough to be heard.

"I guess so. She's in the house."

"Could you ask her to come outside? I'd like to speak to her in private."

Pulling the dog with him, Willis disappeared into the kitchen.

A few minutes later, Sarah showed up. "Good morning, Patrick. I was just thinking about you."

He smiled. "You were?"

"Yes, and I think we should talk."

He nodded. "That's why I'm here. I have something I need to say to you."

"What's that?"

He motioned to a grassy spot near the canal. "Can we go over there and talk?"

"Sure." Sarah followed him across the grass, and they took seats on a couple of boulders.

"What'd you want to say?" Sarah asked.

He moistened his lips with the tip of his tongue. "Well, I've been thinkin' about my marriage proposal."

"I've been thinking about it, too, and I've reached a decision."

"Before you tell me what you've decided, there's something I need to say first."

"What's that?"

"If you agree to marry me, then it'll have to be on one condition."

"What condition?"

"You'll have to get rid of that yappy dog."

Sarah's face blanched. "That's not going to happen, Patrick."

"You mean you won't get rid of the dog?"

"No, and I'm not going to marry you."

"Because the dog doesn't like me? Is that the reason?"

"Of course not."

"Then it's the kids, isn't it? I'm sure they don't like me either."

Sarah nibbled on her bottom lip. "The thing is . . . my kids loved their papa, and I don't think they're ready for me to get married again. Especially not to someone—"

"If the kids weren't in the picture, then would you marry me?"

Sarah scowled at him. "I'd never abandon my kids for any man!"

His face heated. "I'm not askin' you to leave your kids. I just wondered if things were different, and you didn't have any kids, would you have said yes to my proposal?"

Sarah slowly shook her head. "I don't think so, Patrick. You're a nice man, but you're not a committed Christian, and—"

"I've been goin' to church almost every Sunday for the past few months. Doesn't that show you something?"

"I know you've been in church, and I'm glad you have, but attending church doesn't make a person a Christian. You have to make a commitment to the Lord, and ask Him to forgive your sins and invite Him into your heart."

"I've been listening to the preacher's sermons, and givin' it some thought. Someday—maybe soon—I might be ready to take that step. Might even let the preacher baptize me in the canal next summer."

Sarah smiled. "I'm glad to hear you're considering that, but please don't do it for me. You have to want it in here." She touched her chest. "You have to want it because you know you need to seek forgiveness for your sins."

He nodded. "I realize that, but once I do become a Christian, will that change your mind about marrying me?"

"I'm sorry, Patrick, but I'm not in love with you, and without love, I'd never marry again." She touched his arm gently. "If you wait and seek God's will, I'm sure you'll find the right woman someday."

Patrick stood, trying to absorb all she'd said. He'd been hoping to get Sarah's answer, and he had. In one way, he felt disappointment. In another way, he felt relief. Maybe in time, he would find someone else, but when he went looking, he'd make sure that the woman he proposed to didn't have a yappy dog.

Chapter 36

"*I*t's sure gotten quiet around here since the canal closed for the winter," Kelly said to Sarah as the two of them sat at Kelly's kitchen table, drinking a cup of tea one Saturday morning in the middle of December.

Sarah nodded and sighed. "It's good not to have to run outside all the time to let boats through the lock, but I'm worried that I won't have enough money to see us through until spring."

"But you don't have to pay Hortence for helping you now that you're here with the kids all day."

"True."

"And you get to live here, rent free."

"Uh-huh."

"Have you been saving some of the money you've made from lock tending?"

Sarah nodded. "Yes, but I've been saving most of it in the hope that someday——"

A knock sounded on the door just then, and Sarah pushed away from the table. "I'd better see who that is."

When Sarah opened the door, her breath caught in her throat. "Elias! I . . . I thought you'd left the canal."

"I did, but I came back." He leaned against the doorjamb as though needing some support.

"We heard you sold your boat."

"That's true. I sold it to someone who doesn't have a home and wants to live on it all year."

"Oh, I see. What about Ned and your mule driver?"

"Ned's staying at the boardinghouse right now, and I sent Frank home with some money so his mother can feed her family while Frank goes to school." He motioned to the horse and buckboard secured to a nearby tree. "If you're not busy right now, I'd like to take you and the kids for a ride."

Sarah tipped her head. "Where would we go?"

"It's a surprise."

Sarah wasn't sure what to think of Elias's sudden arrival or of the fact that he wanted them to take a ride with him on this cold, snowy day, but she nodded agreeably and said, "Let's go inside and get the kids."

As soon as they entered the kitchen, the children left their seats at the table and swarmed around Elias.

"It's so good to see ya!" Sammy said, when Elias gave them all a hug. "Are ya back for good?"

"I hope so, but it'll depend on how things go." Elias looked over at Kelly and winked. At least Sarah thought it was a wink. Maybe he just had a snowflake stuck to his lashes.

"Elias wants to take us for a ride in his buckboard," Sarah said to the children. "So if you want to go, you'd better hurry and get your coats."

The children let out a whoop and raced upstairs. They were back in a few minutes, bundled up and wearing excited expressions.

Kelly rose from her seat. "I'd better get back to the store. I left the kids in Mike's charge, and if things have gotten busy, he might need my help." She smiled at Elias. "It's nice seeing you, and I hope things work out just the way you want."

Sarah got her coat, and then everyone filed out the door. While Elias helped Sarah and the kids into the buggy, Kelly headed for home.

"Where we goin'?" Willis asked, leaning over the seat back and tapping Elias's shoulder.

Elias grinned. "It's a secret, but we'll be there soon, and then you can tell me what you think."

"What we think about what?" Sarah asked.

"You'll see."

A short time later, Elias guided his horse and wagon into town and pulled up in front of a large, wooden building with two front doors facing the street.

"Here we are," he said, guiding the horse to the hitching rail.

"What are we doing at Martha's boarding-house?" Sarah asked.

"It's not hers anymore," Elias said. "Martha moved to Easton to live near Bobby and his folks, and I bought Martha's place. Ned's staying here right now, but eventually he'll need to move."

Sarah stared at the building, then back at Elias. "Why would you buy a boardinghouse?"

"Are ya gonna live in town and let folks stay with ya?" Sammy asked.

Elias shook his head. "No, not at all." He pointed to the first door. "That one's the entrance to the newspaper office I'll soon be opening." He grinned at Sarah and then pointed to the other door. "That one's for you."

"For me?" Sarah's forehead wrinkled. "What are you talking about, Elias?"

"The downstairs is for your new bakery, and the upstairs can be your home."

"My . . . my bakery? My home?" she murmured.

He nodded. "Carolyn told me that she'd suggested the idea of a bakery to you, and that you seemed interested. She also explained that the reason you said no to my proposal wasn't because of the ugly red mark on my face, but because I was a boatman."

"That's true." She leaned closer and touched the side of his face. "Your birthmark has never bothered me. All I've ever seen when I've looked at you is your kind, gentle spirit."

Elias took both of Sarah's hands and held them in his. "Since I knew you wanted a fresh start, I used the money I got from the sale of my boat and bought this building."

Sarah sat in stunned silence. She'd never imagined that Elias would do such a thing.

"Would you say something, Sarah? Will you take the gift I'm offering?"

"Oh, Elias," she finally squeaked. "I couldn't accept such a generous gift."

"Why not?"

"It wouldn't look right for a widowed woman to accept an expensive gift from a man who's not even a family member."

"I think we could remedy that," Elias said with a twinkle in his eyes.

"Oh?"

He leaned close. So close that Sarah could feel his warm breath tickle the back of her neck. "Carolyn said you'd written and told her that you're not going to marry Patrick."

"That's correct. It wouldn't be right for me to marry a man I don't love."

Elias sat for several seconds; then he turned to her and said, "I love you, Sarah, and if you'll agree to marry me, then no one can say anything about you accepting an expensive gift from your husband."

"Yes! Yes!" Sammy shouted from the rear seat. "Say yes, Mama. Tell Elias that you'll marry him!"

Tearfully, and with a heart full of joy, Sarah nodded her head. "I love you, too, Elias, and I'm more than willing to become your wife."

Elias smiled and then looked over his shoulder at the children. "Turn your heads for a minute, please."

"How come?" Helen wanted to know.

"Because I'm going to kiss your mama."

Helen giggled and turned her head. The boys did the same. Then Elias slowly lowered his head and captured Sarah's lips in a kiss so gentle and sweet that she thought she might swoon.

Thunderous applause erupted behind them. Sarah, her cheeks growing warm, pulled slowly away from Elias and turned around. All three children wore wide smiles as they bobbed their heads in approval.

"We're gonna get a new pa!" Sammy shouted. "And we all love him so much!"

"Yes, we certainly do," Sarah said as she clasped Elias's hand.

Just then, Pastor William came running down the street, his eyes wide, as he waved his hands.

Sarah's heart gave a lurch. Had something terrible happened?

"I knew you were going to be here showing Sarah the building you'd bought," Pastor William said, stepping up to the buggy. "So I had to come and tell you the good news."

More good news? Sarah could hardly contain herself.

"What is it?" Elias asked before Sarah could voice the question.

"The doctor's with Betsy, and she's just given birth to a baby boy!" Pastor William's smile widened. "We've decided to name him Hiram

Abel Covington, after Betsy's father. Betsy thinks we should call him Abe, though. He'll probably like that better than Hiram."

Sarah smiled. "Congratulations! Tell Betsy I'll be over to see her and the baby as soon as she's had a chance to rest up."

"I will." Pastor William looked at Elias. "How's it going here?"

"She's agreed to become my wife." Elias grinned and lifted Sarah's hand. "We'll soon be running our businesses side by side."

"I'm happy it's all worked out. Congratulations to you both." Pastor William motioned to the parsonage down the street. "I'd better get home. See you all in church on Sunday!"

As Pastor William sprinted toward home, Sarah sat staring at the side of the building that would soon be her new home and place of business. Apparently Pastor William, and perhaps even Kelly, had been in on Elias's little secret.

Sarah's heart overflowed with so much happiness that she thought it might burst. She reflected on the verse of scripture Pastor William had shared with the congregation the previous Sunday, Philippians 4:19: *"But my God shall supply all your need according to his riches in glory by Christ Jesus."* She knew with certainty that when God brought Elias Brooks into her life, He'd supplied all of her and the children's needs.

Epilogue

Six months later

*A*s Sarah worked contentedly in her bakery, a deep sense of peace welled in her soul. Not only was her new business venture working out well, but it gave her such joy knowing that her husband was happily working in his newspaper office next door. She no longer had to worry about her children living too close to the canal, nor about them growing up and being forced to work on the canal.

She grabbed a hunk of dough and began kneading it. So much had happened in the last six months. She and Elias had gotten married in the church here in Walnutport, and then Elias had taken her and the children to Easton to meet his family. Afterward, they'd gone to Roger and Mary's house to see Maria. Sarah was pleased at how well Maria was doing. Even though her sight had gotten worse, she seemed happy, and Mary was obviously taking good care of her.

Another thing that had happened after Sarah and Elias got married was that Ned had moved into the lock tender's house and taken over the responsibility of raising and lowering the lock. He seemed quite content with his new job, and often said he didn't miss riding on the boat at all.

Carolyn, too, had a new job. She'd left her old teaching position in Easton and moved to Walnutport to take over Mabel Clark's position, because Mabel had gotten married and moved to New York. Carolyn seemed happy teaching here, and of course, second-grader Sammy and Willis, who was now in the first grade, were thrilled to have Elias's sister as their new teacher.

Hortence, who'd been sure that she would always be single, had married Sam Abernathy, one of the farmers who lived in the area, and she seemed very content.

Two more surprising things had happened: Elias had made peace with his father, who was delighted when he heard that Elias had opened his own newspaper. Then there was Patrick, who'd recently given his heart to the Lord and had begun courting Carolyn.

Sarah smiled. She'd never imagined Carolyn and Patrick together, but then a year ago, she'd never dreamed that she'd be married to Elias, or that she'd be living in town, doing something she enjoyed.

"Umm . . . something smells awfully good in here," Elias said as he stepped into the bakery. "Have you got anything I can sample this morning?"

She swatted his hand playfully as he reached out to grab one of the oatmeal cookies cooling on a wire rack. "What are you doing over here? I thought you'd be hard at work in your office."

"I was, but I got hungry and knew you'd have something I could eat."

She chuckled and handed him a cookie.

"Are you happy, Mrs. Brooks?" he murmured against her ear.

"Oh yes, very much so."

Elias turned Sarah to face him and kissed the tip of her nose. "I've never been happier than I am being married to you, and I hope you have no regrets."

"None at all." Sarah leaned into his embrace and closed her eyes. She knew without a doubt that she had made the right choice. Elias was everything she could want in a husband, and what a wonderful father he was to her children. Someday, Lord willing, they might have a child or two of their own. In the meantime, she was going to enjoy every day the Lord gave her as Mrs. Elias Brooks.

RECIPE FOR SARAH'S DOUGH DAB

Ingredients:
4 cups flour
1 teaspoon salt
½ cup lard or shortening
5 teaspoons baking powder
Milk

Stir dry ingredients in a bowl with a spoon. Add enough milk to make a stiff dough. Roll out on a floured board and cut into round pieces. Put in a greased frying pan and fry until done. Turn as you would for a pancake. Brown on both sides, then serve as a bread substitute.

Author's Note

*T*he Lehigh Navigation System was completed in 1829, and boats began using the entire length of it by 1832. The canal era reached its peak in 1850, and continued to diminish until it came to an end in 1931. Today, visitors can still experience some of those exciting canal days at the Canal Museum in Easton, Pennsylvania. There's also a restored canal boat pulled by two mules that can be ridden at the Hugh Moore Park, which is also in Easton. The restored lock tender's house in Walnutport is another interesting place to visit, and of course, it's always fun to walk the towpath where the steady *clip-clop* of mule teams used to be heard. Whenever I'm in Pennsylvania, I always enjoy visiting various sections of the Lehigh Canal and reliving in my mind the glory of the canal era. For more information on the Lehigh Navigation System visit www.canals.org.

About the Author

WANDA E. BRUNSTETTER is a bestselling author who enjoys writing historical, as well as Amish-themed novels. Wanda's interest in the Lehigh Canal began when she married her husband, Richard, who grew up in Pennsylvania, near the canal. Wanda and Richard have made numerous trips to Pennsylvania, where they have several friends and relatives. They've walked the towpath, ridden on a canal boat, and toured the lock tender's house. Wanda hopes her readers will enjoy this historical series as much as she enjoyed researching and writing it.

Wanda and her husband have two grown children and six grandchildren. In her spare time, Wanda enjoys photography, ventriloquism, gardening, reading, stamping, and having fun with her family.

In addition to her novels, Wanda has written two Amish cookbooks, two Amish devotionals, several Amish children's books, as well as numerous novellas, stories, articles, poems, and puppet scripts.

Visit Wanda's Web site at www.wanda brunstetter.com and feel free to e-mail her at wanda@wandabrunstetter.com.

Center Point Publishing
600 Brooks Road ● PO Box 1
Thorndike ME 04986-0001 USA

(207) 568-3717

US & Canada:
1 800 929-9108
www.centerpointlargeprint.com